T0082620

# Finding God's Vision for Your Life

# FINDING GOD'S VISION FOR YOUR LIFE

SUSAN SYKES

**FINDING GOD'S VISION FOR YOUR LIFE**



*iUniverse books may be ordered through booksellers or by contacting:*

*iUniverse*
*1663 Liberty Drive*
*Bloomington, IN 47403*
*www.iuniverse.com*
*844-349-9409*



*ISBN: 978-1-6632-3026-3 (sc)*
*ISBN: 978-1-6632-3027-0 (e)*

*Library of Congress Control Number: 2021920931*

*Print information available on the last page.*

*iUniverse rev. date: 11/04/2021*

# DEDICATION

◇◇◇◇◇◇◇◇◇◇◇◇◇◇◇◇◇◇◇◇◇◇◇◇◇

I would like to thank Jesus Christ who is my Lord and Savior; for keeping me, protecting me, leading, guiding me in the right direction, healing me from past hurts, picking me up and turning my life around. If it had not been for the Lord, my King on my side; I don't know what my life would be like today. I've been through the fire, the storm and the rain but He kept me, through it all. That's why I learned to trust in Jesus Christ, through it all. How great is my God? His name is above every other name on this earth and I give Him all the praise, the glory and I will worship Him forever and ever. His grace is amazing to me, I once was lost, I was blind but now I see and understand things much better. I would like to thank all the churches I attended, Bible classes at a few churches and all the wonderful Pastors that teach the word of God and whose souls were on fire for Jesus Christ. Thanks for being leaders, being good followers, being obedient and being faithful to God's word. It helped me mature, love like God (the agape love), walk in the light, walk in the newness of life and be like Him more and more each day. Susan's vision is much clearer and brighter today.

I also dedicate this book to my parents, Evelyn E. Brown, and Charles Brown, Jr. My dad is no longer here but he's in my heart. I want to thank them, for birthing me into this world. Giving thanks to, Mrs. Evelyn for helping me become the woman I am today. My mom did a wonderful job raising all of her children as a single mother and I love her very much. She loved all her children the same and never took sides. Evelyn just wanted her children to always get along with one another, even if there were any disagreements. She loved a peaceful, warm home and for her children to always love like a family should.

Susan wants to thank her daughter, Bria for helping me see my vision better. She always wanted her own business and never wanted to work for anyone, so that had me thinking. Many of us have gifts but are blind, even when the opportunity is right in your face. We refuse to use our God gifted talents because we don't understand the value in them. Bria enjoys helping people but many are ignorant to the knowledge with which she educates the world. But she never allowed that to stop her from moving on and helping others who wanted more for themselves and their families. Many people have been successful with what she provides. We are moving, working, towards our dreams and goals. I want everyone who believes they are entitled to having an abundant life, to go for it. To have wealth because it was meant for many to be successful and not struggle for the rest of their lives. That is what Bria does, help people, and as a mother I am very proud of her.

I want to thank the Lord for my husband, Kenneth. We had been through dark roads, had to climb the mountains and had up and downs but we give thanks to our Lord and Savior Jesus Christ. If I never had a problem, I would never realize that God was able to fix what was broken and could provide healing. The Holy Spirit has shown me how to handle many situations, through the word of God. That's why I will bless the Lord at all times. I also want to thank my stepmother, Ethel for being there when me and my husband needed her. I want to thank my son, granddaughter, stepchildren, family members, friends and everyone who reads this book for supporting me and showing their love. I pray that you all start thinking and be able to get a vision, that will help you live the life you always dreamed of and enjoy a vision that you could have never imagined. Be Blessed!

# CONTENTS

◇◇◇◇◇◇◇◇◇◇◇◇◇◇◇◇◇◇◇◇◇◇◇◇

# PREFACE

◇◇◇◇◇◇◇◇◇◇◇◇◇◇◇◇◇◇◇◇◇◇◇◇◇◇

This book is designed to help people to not struggle, to make peace with all men, get a vision, a goal, dream big dreams, overcome hatred, acknowledge your gifts and God given talents and use them wisely and to the glory of God. Make better choices, have a backup plan, think big, get unstuck, don't be afraid to fail but believe in yourself. Always know what is your why. Your WHY, is going to take you place you never dreamed of going. Susan experienced not having a vision for years. She knew she wanted nice things: a nice home and money, where she wouldn't have to work when she got older. People don't realize the value of time and how much money they need at retirement. You need a lot of money and Susan found out once she got older that what she needed was to have a plan, a goal, get a vision and have your own business. As she looked at so many people who struggled when the Coronavirus hit, in March of 2020, many didn't have three to six months of living expenses set aside, no money saved, they couldn't pay their bills and had no plan in place. Remember, there are many older people who are still working because they have to. We learned nothing about money in school and the fact of the matter is, we need money for everything we do.

The world is divided: no love for one another, killing, people are disrespectful, and we need more love and a vision. A vision for the world to heal, overcome hate, equal opportunities and have peace everywhere. Families need to start talking with their loved ones and learn to build a business. Bring in a good amount of money, learn to invest and save. Get a business that others can benefit from and leave an inheritance for your children. Sadly, though, many people don't talk about dreams, goals and money. They just spend every little bit they have and leave nothing to fall back on. Take a look right now at your life. How many years have you been working? How much money do you have saved up or invested, from all those years? Many have worked all our lives and have nothing to show for it -- many don't have even a hundred dollars or a thousand dollars saved. We are time broke or money broke. Get a vision, find a need and fill it; help others learn to do better. Do good, better and your best. We are used to working for others making them rich. Let's get unstuck and do better financially.

# INTRODUCTION

◇◇◇◇◇◇◇◇◇◇◇◇◇◇◇◇◇◇◇◇◇◇◇

I would like to welcome you all to my book, called "Finding God's Vision for Your Life." What's holding you back? The reason why I am writing this book is to help as many people as I can to start living their dreams, get a goal, and have a clear vision. And, most importantly, to accept Jesus Christ as your Lord and Savior to help you with your journey to victory! You will find that both nowadays and years ago many of us never dreamed of having a business or a vision. By reading some of the stories and relationship stories in this book, He will show you, your vision and help it come to life. Some people never try to work together as a family or have a family business. Think about someone you know who you can trust, get along with, is truthful and you all come up with a plan to have your own business. You can do it, if you put your mind into it, if you try diligently and remain steadfast in your determination to succeed. This is something many of us never do with our family or loved ones. We as a family always sit down and talk about many things, but never about a business. We never talk about money as a team, how we can all be successful together, helping each other, planning, sticking together and working as one united family.

We sit at home watch TV, watch movies, watch basketball, football, we talk together, laugh together, cry together, drink, get drunk together and sometimes talk about one another, instead of being happy for a love ones, etc. And none of these things help bring more money or give us what we need to survive. And the Coronavirus, Black Lives Matter and all this killing in 2020 doesn't help. But with God's agape kind of love, we can help the world pull these things together. Being together with family Is great but how are our family circumstances; why or why not? Are they getting better with dreams; why or why not? Are our finances getting better; why? Are our family relationships getting better? Look at the world around us, it's really time for a change. Do we have enough to pay our bills or are we just barely making ends meet? Put your minds together and think. It's time to do some amazing things and make this world a better place.

We cheer other famous people on but we have no plans lined up for ourselves or the family. Do you have a backup plan if your job lays you off or the place where you are employed closes down? Many feel they can never own their own business or have people working for them. Well, no one said it would be easy but I want to encourage you to put your best into something you would truly like to do. Get your own business going now and work hard for yourself. Until your money starts working for you, and then you won't have to work so hard. Your money will roll in while you relax and do what you love to do. You have to get people's attention, have them interested in what you do. Once you start your vision, say to yourself: I got this! People may try to knock you down but keep moving, keep smiling. Nothing means as much as your smile, and when you smile, know that everything is going to be alright. When you smile, hold your head up, stand tall, spread your wings and fly.

Are you afraid to make that move toward success? If you want a better life, live better, make the money you really need, teach your children how to carry your family legacy on or your legacy, we must teach each other, work together and bring a new reality into existence (to continue on). We all need a financial coach. That's because, as soon as things start coming alive, working out great, the devil will come and try to control your mind. (James 4:7) Therefore submit to God. Resist the devil and he will flee from you. Satan doesn't like when you have faith and believe in yourself. The devil loves to divide families, marriages and relationships. (Ephesians 4:27) nor give place to the devil. Avoid letting Satan keep controlling your thought life, thinking patterns, and your mind because he will continue to take over your life. He will keep you in bondage and stop you from receiving all your blessings. All good things come from heaven above; not from the devil. You will need God in your life, in order to be more successful and have better results. He will show you your vision and what to do/what not to do. He is our best teacher, leader, our strength, our helper and our healer. He gives us power and He will show you things that you never thought you could do. We must be able to try something new, step out on faith and believe God is who He said He is and can do what He says He can do. Be blessed, do your best, don't stress, get rest. It's only a test and you will steadily become better in everything you do. Pray, get a vision and dream big, big, big dreams. Stop waiting. Now is the time.

# What's Holding You Back?

◇◇◇◇◇◇◇◇◇◇◇◇◇◇◇◇◇◇◇◇◇◇◇◇◇

Find ways to get a vision and stop procrastinating. Are you living a miserable, broke life? Living paycheck to paycheck. You are not alone, many of us are in the same situation. Susan experienced these things too! Many males/females are in a bad relationship/marriage and can't see their way out…are you one of them? Well, you are not alone! Who are you letting stop you from getting ahead? A lot of people get excited about knowledge that a professional business man/woman gives to them and explains how the business works. They taught you how to be independent, and you got so excited. You wanted to do it because it sounded good, you could survive at retirement, take care of the family much better, pay cash for everything you purchase and take trips. Wealthy people travel, don't have to answer to anyone, send their kids to college and it is good for all the people in the world to become independent. Later you tell the business person, "let me think about it" and either you thought about it too long, or you didn't think at all, and the more days that go by you grow less interested. Or you went home to your family, you were so excited and on fire to get the business rolling. You mentioned it to everyone in the family. The mother, friends, family members, girlfriend, boyfriend, father, aunt, uncle, wife or husband -- and they all talked you out of doing the business/goal. This is such a big mistake! Never let anyone talk you out of something you know is right for you, your future dream and the family. You are grown and you should know if something will take care of you for the rest of your life and if it makes plenty of sense to you.

Many have let a loved one, or someone they love, husband, wife, mother and father, tell them not to do something that they know will build wealth to their life. You have let them stop you; now you have to stay on the time clock for the rest of your life. Again, you're not alone! Ironically, those are the main people who should be by your side, especially if everyone in the world needs it or can benefit from your business. Broke people who are in the same boat you are in. Avoid listening to them and decide for yourself. Most people are afraid to try new things or own a business, something that could be owned by you. Abusive relationships can blind our view, and keep us from looking forward to something great. Hanging with the wrong people/crowds, in the wrong place and having no positive people to back you up, that can be a distraction and hold you back. The ones that get you in trouble and they put the blame on you all the time, avoid them. Doing things that you know aren't right but you do it anyway so you can have friends. You have no goals, no back up plan or vision. God can help pull you out of any situation that is not good for your soul. (James 4:8) Draw near to God and He will draw near to you. Cleanse your hands, you sinners; and purify your hearts, you double-minded people. Jesus Christ might be that puzzle piece which is missing in your life; not worldly people. We are here to help win lost souls (sinners), to Jesus Christ. We all want to be loved and would like to have a better life. Dream big and get a vision. (Acts 2:17) It is time to start living the dreams you always wanted. Think for yourself, let that person be mad but when they see you are building wealth, what can they say then? Professional people are here to help you and not criticize you. Just listen, it might just help you make the right choices. Stop letting people tell you what and what not to do; you have nothing to lose but you can gain so much more for your life and for your family.

# VISION

◇◇◇◇◇◇◇◇◇◇◇◇◇◇◇◇◇◇◇◇◇◇◇◇◇◇◇◇

"Turning dreams, wishes, and goals into a future vision." It is important to have a vision, purpose and a passion for your future. Joseph in a dream (Matthew 2:13). Sometimes we have to depart from things in order to see the vision/plan that God should have us to follow. Start planning while you are young, in school and in college because "after that it's adult living." A time to grow up, mature and have a dream, goals that will last a lifetime. Everything has a time (Ecclesiastes 3:1-8) and to everything there is a season, a time for every purpose under heaven. A time to be born/born again, a time to die, A time to plant, A time to pluck what is planted, A time to kill (get rid of) and a time to heal. God wants us all to have peace and see clearly. Without Him we are nothing, can't do anything and we are lost. We need His word to wake us up, wake up wake up; we have a big job to do for Jesus Christ. What we do for Christ is everlasting and will last a lifetime. (Isaiah 65:17), All earthly things will pass away and are not forever. (Matthew 24:35). The heaven and earth will pass away, but God's words shall not pass away. Life is very short.

God has good things in store for everyone. It will support your family and yourself for the rest of your life. Make sure you have all your family values in place. Saving money in the bank won't earn a lot of interest on your money but it's a start to open an account. That way you will have something in place, as a starter. Have life insurance, money saved for an emergency, identity theft, investments such as a 401k or a Roth IRA, and a Will. You will need a professional coach. These are things men/women don't have and feel nothing is going to happen to them. People's lives are taken daily; not one life but three to five almost every day. And now that the Coronavirus is here, March 2020 it has gotten worse. It has affected the whole world. Many people feel that these things are not important and that they are here on earth forever. In order to make dreams come true! Wake up, see the light, get directions, get the big picture, we have been in the darkness too long. It seems like a dark road because people are holding on to the past, unforgiving spirit and procrastinating. Many people go by their feelings and never let go of the pain from inside of them. There is a bright light at the end of the road. It is never too late, go for it now. Let nothing hold you back.

Some people know what they would like to become and a lot of us have no idea. Others found out when they get older, like in their 40s or 50s and some never find their way. Many women/men have talent but refuse to use the gifts that God gave them. Don't neglect your gifts, we all can do great things in life. Some of us have many gifts but are scared to practice them, or to even sit down and discuss it, (1 Timothy 4:14). You can't wait for someone else to do something, you have to go after your goal and follow your dreams. (James 1:17). Start early, make the right decisions that will help you retire early in life. Making a very good salary or bringing in a nice amount of income so you can enjoy retirement, that will make a big difference in the years to come. Have a nice home, home paid off, vehicles paid off, no credit card bills, being debt free, take trips and relax, this is what you should want, after working for years. Never depend on a person because they can and will walk right out of your life. Always have your own, make your own money because you never know when you will be alone. You will never know when that job will let you go. Jobs only care about you getting the work done, and want to pay you as little as possible... while they become rich. Get yourself a professional coach, who can help you manage/budget your money. A coach can show/teach you things you never knew. Never let anyone shoot you down. Follow your dreams, if it will benefit you. Please use your gifts (James 1:17). Every good gift and every perfect gift are from above and comes down from the Father of lights, with whom there is no variation or shadow of turning.

Many visions come from dreams and having a need to help others. Get a vision, have a plan, a purpose, a passion, and why you think it would be a good idea. Know your why. (2 Corinthians 13:9). You should have a burning desire, strong emotions, have good support and believe in yourself, that you can do it. Your mother and dad should each be one of the main people who support you and cheer you on. When people cheer together; they can win together. God want us to have an abundant life and showing love to all people. (John 10:10) The thief does not come except to steal and to kill, and to destroy. "I (God) have come that they may have life and that they may have it more abundantly." When you have a vision, things will begin to change, nothing stays the same in life anyway. There will always be changes going on around you, as you start aging and in your life. As you can see this world has changed dramatically right before our eyes. As of March 3, 2020, the Coronavirus is rampaging all across the world. No one was prepared for this sickness and many don't have 6 months to 12 months of emergency money saved or invested for a disaster like this. The change will depend on your thinking, a mind change, your heart needs to be right and the people you choose to hang around makes a big difference when it comes to your success as well. We must have a backup plan, so when trouble comes, we are financially stable. The Coronavirus caught everyone off guard in 2020. That was a smack in the face.

Be careful of the people you spend time with and who you call friends, depending on their character you don't necessarily want to turn out to be like them. Friends, how many of us have them? I mean true friends, the ones on whom we can depend. What you follow, who you are following and who you listen to, will determine your future. Stop being afraid to try new things or something different. Have faith, believe in yourself and you will not regret that move. Read, (Proverbs 23:7) "as a man think in his heart so shall he be." Do what's on your mind; there are so many things in life that can keep the mind away from moving into victory. Where you came from, the area you live in, being poor, or middle class (not too poor) doesn't mean you have to stay that way. There are some rich people who make big money, but many are not happy; others have no money saved because they just like to spend it. Some have money saved, and they have a professional coach who helps teach them about where to put their money, so it can grow. You can make changes as you get older and can be happy. Your mind is a terrible thing to waste or damage! Have a mind like Christ, and if you have a partner make sure you both are on the same track and headed in the same direction. Or you are going to have problems. (Romans 12:16) Be of the same mind toward one another. Do not set your mind on high things, but associate with the humble. Do not be wise in your own opinion. Go to God, your Helper, and make sure you pray to Him for the best answer. Be that light, life, and salt to the world and shine brightly.

# Vocabulary

◇◇◇◇◇◇◇◇◇◇◇◇◇◇◇◇◇◇◇◇◇◇◇◇◇

Afraid—filled with regret or concern

Begin—to start something

Burning desire---a strong wish, wanting something badly

Commitment—to do, carry out

Create—to make, to bring something into existence

Darkness---without light

Determined---having firmly made up your mind

Fear---the feeling of being afraid

Focus---to adjust the lens (eyes), get the clear picture

Forgive---to stop being angry with somebody for something they have done wrong

Great---very large, important and famous, very good

Hatred---a strong dislike

Hidden---go somewhere you cannot be seen

Ignorant---not knowing about something

Lifestyle—the way you live your life

Listen---to pay attention so that you can hear something

Love---to care for somebody or something very much, a strong feeling of liking somebody

Mature---fully grown or developed

Motivated---having a reason to do something

Opportunities—a chance to do something

Pleasure---a feeling of joy and happiness

Pointless----no clue

Remove---to take away

Serious---not laughing or joking

Strong---powerful not weak

Tough---not easily broken or damaged, able to endure hardship, illness

Weak---not strong

# Question--What is your why?

Women and men; what is your vision? If you don't have a goal, why? Your why is very important. Think about something you really would enjoy doing. Something that can touch people's lives and it would help them live a better life. You want to try and help all people to not make the mistakes you made. Many of us wait too long to make a move because we are so used to and settled into our old ways of life. Why is it so hard to change and do better? Are you letting someone control you? Do you have imposter syndrome? Susan in her past felt imposter syndrome but once she listened to how some of the successful people shared their story she came out of her shell and shyness. Many felt the same way Susan was feeling. Susan felt she wasn't good enough to own a business and become successful, and she was afraid to speak out because she didn't know what people would say about her.

God has put something in all of us and we all can have what successful people have. We just have to copy what they do and stay focused. We must pull down those strongholds and move obstacles out of our way. Put an end to the problems and other things that are blocking your way. Always get to the root of the problem and dig deep. You could be holding yourself back from a blessing. Take a look at yourself in the mirror. It could be a jealous partner who's in your way.

There are so many gorgeous women out here and some make more money than their soul mate and the men are jealous of that woman. You have her, so why be mad; if you don't like it, leave her alone. There are plenty other men who are waiting for her to be single. Men/women, be very careful of a jealous male/female, watch their emotions because they kill people faster than anyone else. Have a mate who's willing to support you with your goals/dreams. It's good to read and study the Bible. It's here to heal the soul, and encourage you to do awesome things in life. Never harm an individual you love because you don't want to deal with the consequences; you must to walk away. Negative thinking can spoil your hopes for the future. Instead, turn your focus always toward the Healer, which is Jesus. Hold on, be strong because help is on the way. Let's get started toward our goal for the future because the next day is not promise to anyone. Many people have passed away due to the Coronavirus in 2020. That could have caused some people's visions to crumble. It is easy to stay stuck in bondage and never experience unique things. But that is not God's way! He gave all of us a body, a voice, and He wants us to make a powerful impact in other's people lives.

Answer the following questions to start you on your journey to success.

Do you have a vision or dream? What is it?

What is your purpose or need for it?

Do you have a passion for the vision or dream?

What is your why?

Are you on the mission to your victory?

Have you ever thought about having your own business?

Do you want to work for people for the rest of your life?

How is your attitude? A good attitude can take you many places in life.

What's stopping you from reaching your goal or vision?

Have you ever tried God? Be committed to God and watch Him move in your life.

Have you ever sat down with someone and had a conversation about your own business or family business?

Have you ever talked about creating Wealth for yourself or the family?

# Wake Up, Wake Up, Wake Up, To Vision

◇◇◇◇◇◇◇◇◇◇◇◇◇◇◇◇◇◇◇◇◇◇◇◇◇

Women and Men, when you get sick and tired of doing things your way and it's not working, find Jesus Christ. Go to Him in prayer, "asking for help, for a vision, a plan and purpose for your life." We can have a plan and vision for our self but sometimes it just doesn't work out. That's because God has something better in store. There will be a time in our life, where we have to walk only with God, and no one else. Everyone will not be able to go where you go. Some will talk about you, there will be jealousy, they won't help you, hope you don't make it and they surely never thought you would be the one to ever think about becoming a successful person. They stop speaking to you, in fact they don't even want to look at you, and why? Precisely because you are trying to do something great. Many people may have said they would help you but just because others started talking negative about your career, they also turned their backs on you too. They try to stay out of your way, ducking you out because they lied and said they would support you, and on and it goes... but it's ok. Never let anyone stop you from going for what yours, not your vision or your dreams. Go for the goal and become successful in everything you do. What God has for you, it is indeed only for you.

Work hard toward your career and be determined to make things happen. The people that aren't treating you the way you should be treated; get away from them. You deserve better, stop settling for less or thinking you are less of a women or man. Move forward, dream big and make it come to life and into the light. Let your light shine in positive ways and your life will be changed for the best. There are people who God sent your way but you rejected them, procrastinating. Some people think they know everything, so stop listening to unprofessional loved ones and friends or someone who told you it isn't going to work. Stop letting your vision be quashed by inconsiderate people who either purposely or inadvertently belittle your hopes and dreams.

People come in your life for all kinds of reasons, don't miss out on your blessing. Some are there to help wake you up because you can't see clearly. Each one of us has chosen a job, business, career training, took classes, got your license, read books, listened to other professionals, learned from millionaires, or got educated on what they teach or the work they do. So why listen to a person who took no classes, has no knowledge, is not a professional, has never been educated on what someone else knows, doesn't have a license, etc.? Instead, the wise move would be to carefully absorb the teachings of professional people are who are sharing information for free with all people. They are not trying to rush people into doing something but want to share with you some very important knowledge that they themselves once never knew. They want to share how it helped them and other people who they have helped. They want to help you grow your money and help your family be set for life. They don't think they are better than others, because there's some business people who will charge you a nice price for the free information. I'm talking about magnanimous folks who are trying to give you free knowledge so you can grow and understand what is really going on in life. Stop being rude, thinking you know everything. Read books and be open to free information, what do you have to lose? Try it and see if it will get you somewhere in life and make you successful. If it is not for you, pass it on to others.

Help people who try to help you because you might someday get a business and would want people to support what you do! Especially if it is a family member. If you help people become independent, you can't stop yourself from becoming successful and independent. Do you want freedom? Many people listen to strangers, so what's wrong with a loved one who knows what they are talking about and wants to help you. People purchase books and courses and products from strangers who get over on them, tell them lies and many of us doesn't realize what they have or how things work with their coverage or products. Because they don't read the fine print; meaning those tiny small words at the bottom. Many of us have supported and received items, coverage and have purchased things from others but not from your own family members. Always support your family! You have everything to gain, especially when you don't like what you currently do. You will be surprised to know what is inside of you and what you can do.

"Never let broke people talk you out of something." Are they helping you, paying your bills and putting food on the table? Once you start making money, then they will be looking at you basically saying, "Well, I tried to talk you out of it but I am glad you kept going!" Anybody can do whatever they put their mind to. Why do you think it is impossible to become a millionaire or to have billions? Is it because that is how the mind has been programmed from years ago, back in the 1920s? Stop thinking small and go after the abundant life, so you can live a better life and have peace. There are plenty of opportunities that are available for you right now. Learn to get wisdom and knowledge, and avoid being ignorant when people want to share with you how to be motivated. Yes, everything is not for everybody but try new opportunities. People perish because of a lack of knowledge. Read: Hosea 4:6. In all your ways acknowledge Him. And He shall direct your paths. (Proverbs 3:6).

# Mary Growing Up

Mary's mom, named Shelly, was married to her dad but got a divorce years later. Shelly didn't know how she was going to provide for her six children. She did know that God was amongst them. She had a vision to have her own business someday but her mind was telling her, your dreams are gone. How are you going to do it without income from your ex-husband? The little voice in her head told Shelly it's impossible for you to achieve that goal. Shelly began to doubt her belief and would cry at night, while the children were asleep. The next morning Shelly was fixing breakfast and Mary walked into the kitchen. She saw that her mother's eyes were red and puffy. Mary asked, "Mom, is something wrong?"

Shelly replied, "No, sweetheart, everything is fine."

The girl told her, "Mom, you haven't been the same since Dad left. It's been two years, Mom, and maybe you need to start dating."

"I don't know if that's a good idea," Shelly replied.

"Sure it is, Mom! You need to go out and enjoy yourself. When was the last time you went out?"

Shelly smiled. "I have no clue, but it's been a while."

Mary said, "Mom, you always told us to pray and you need to pray."

"You are right, Mary! I am going to go pray and have a long talk with my Savior."

Mary said, "You're looking better already." She gave her mom a kiss on the cheek and went back upstairs saying, "Mom, let me know when you finish cooking."

Shelly said, "I will!" and then looked up at the ceiling and smiled, adding, "Thank You, Jesus."

Months later, Shelly started dating for a while; until she found Tom. Growing up as child, Mary and her other sibling had much fun and they lived in Virginia. She remembered Mr. Tom taking her to school, which was in a trailer home. Trailer homes and small buildings that didn't look like a school but that was how they were back then. Almost every day Mary's mother's boyfriend would take Mary to school. She was so embarrassed because of the work he did, which made his clothes dirty. He wore his work clothes and would get out of the car, kiss her and say, "I will see you later." She didn't want the other children to see the dirty clothes he had on but she didn't understand, Tom was going back to work once he dropped her off. Mary was his favorite little girl. He brought her a rabbit one day and the rabbit wasn't there longer than a week. Mary didn't know what happened to the bunny. She looked all over the house for the rabbit; even in the toilet but never found it. Mary had a dream that her rabbit ran away and found his family and was happy. She would tell her mother Shelly about that story and her mom would smile and give her a hug. About a month later, Mr. Tom brought the kids a puppy named Pooch. They were happy and loved their doggie. Everything was going well with Mr. Tom there. They lived near Mr. Tom's mother house; all you had to do was look out the back door, down the dirt pathway and you could see Kelly's house. Ms. Kelly was Tom's mother. She was a nice old lady, and treated Mary and her siblings like her grandchildren. The children would go over Ms. Kelly's house almost every day.

Mary remembered her mother taking on a part-time job. Shelly would work on the lunch truck, on the weekends, giving away food in the neighborhood at one of the parks. She loved helping serve people because that's what God wants His servants to do. Help one another and see the less fortune fed. Many people came to get the bagged lunches on weekends. There would be a long line most of the time, so you had to get there early. Most of the time they always had enough food for everyone; a few times they ran out. It would be a banana, a sandwich, a drink, chips, an orange, maybe an apple and other food, in the bag. It was good if you were hungry and it would fill you up for a few hours, until dinner time. People would get one or two bags and take them home. Many would eat at the place and talk with one another. There was no fighting or pushing, the people waited patiently for their turn. In those days you could leave your car door and house door unlocked. More people rode bikes or walked. Having a car can makes both males and females lazy. We all could use the exercise; it is good for the body overall, and especially the heart.

Everyone was much friendlier and got along. That is how the Bible wants people to live and show respect toward each other. How many remember getting milk delivered to your home or your grand-mom's house? Mary used to give the milk person a cold bottle of water in the summer time. Did your great grandparents make an impact on your life? You should be happy because who knows where you would be today. Give thanks to God and older people, who talk some sense into us. The older generation would say something like this! "Just be thankful, for what you got. No, we may not drive a great big car right now. You may not even have a car at all, but you can still stand tall. Just always be thankful for all that you do have." Did that bring a memory to you? Those were indeed the good old days, good old days. Life was nothing like it is today, all this killing, fighting, disrespectful children, everyone has lost respect for police officers, and the awful virus of 2020 was deadly. Mary had never seen the world change so fast, as she grew older.

Christmas was fine, you didn't get much but they did get necessities and important items that they needed. It wasn't a room filled with gifts but a few for each person and as children we didn't complain. Her mom did the best she could and did a good job for years. The kids in those days were glad they got one or two things they wanted or needed. They thanked God for what their parents were able to buy for them. It wasn't a lot but they appreciated every little thing. As long as they could play with their friends, they were happy. It wasn't a lot of he said / she said stuff, it was let's enjoy our time together, before it is time to go in the house. Children had to enjoy themselves; enjoy yourself, enjoy yourself with me, you had to enjoy yourself. Remember that song? "Enjoy our time while we are young." Most children today never enjoy their life as children. They either have to help raise their younger siblings, or their parents got hooked on substance abuse/drugs. That affects those children's visions and dreams. Many end up in the streets because that's what they have seen others do. A few parents were alcoholics or just chasing behind a man/woman and forgot about their kids. Try to avoid drugs because one hit can change your life and hinder your dream come true. You want to be able to see, keep the path clear and get the big picture of where you want to be in the next four years. Learn young, we are the children/people who God called to make this world a better place, so let's start living, caring, giving; these are the times we should be forgiving each other and have a vision. Let's make this world a better place, if we can. Reach out and touch somebody's hand and make this world a better place if you can.

Back in the day, parents had control of their kids, and other people's children. A country/town would raise the small boys and girls together. The adults were trying to be role models, parents, and a leader to them. Giving them examples to follow and direction that they needed to take. Children had chores to do, some got a little money, some went on a trip for the summer and others got a toy they always wanted. For many, it was a learning experience; where you couldn't get everything you want but what you need. They learned to earn, to work, and that nothing was free. Children were taught to be respectful, helpful, watch what comes out of the mouth, show love, help elders and others. They were able to talk to their parents. And parent were parents and the children stayed in a child's place. Adults didn't like a child looking them in the face while talking to another adult. That was grown folks' business! The law today has boys and girls thinking they can run over the parents and have control over their homes. Adults are not allowed to beat their kids; some need a beating and there are kids who take the law for granted. Because they feel they can talk back to the mom or dad and know they are not going to lay a hand on them.

There are, of course, men and women who have a problem and abuse their kids for no reason which makes it bad for other, good parents, who are trying to teach the children to be well mannered. That is a lowdown dirty shame, the law has made these kids so confused, it is a shame. They've got the adult burning, on fire, wanting to beat some butts, but when something bad happens, the parent just has to live with the blame. Life can try to weigh you down, but let nothing stop you from moving forward. Be strong parents to your kids, not a friend because way too many children are drinking and using drugs with their parents. The kids start having no respect for their parents and other adults when you allow them to use drugs and drink with them. There was none of that back in the day. You got beat down, back in the old days. A good old-fashioned tail whipping. Some children ended up being much wiser from those tail whippings and dreamed big dreams.

Shelly also had a vision to get her license and travel the world with her children. Once evening, Shelly was trying to drive, just around the corner. The kids were all running on the sidewalk following Shelly and yelling, "Go Mom, go Mom!" Once she made it to Mr. Tom's mother's house, Ms. Shelly drove right into the ditch. It was funny and it wasn't. She must have not used her brakes. The kids were laughing on one hand and also hoping their mom was fine. Ms. Shelly was in fact ok, but she never liked to drive and until this day in 2021, she still does not drive. Her daughters always take her places but sometimes she caught the bus. Shelly has been saving very little money for her business, while Tom is still there.

One day the children in the neighborhood were playing together, and they ran into Maxine, who was a big girl and tall. Maxine would be outside preaching about God and wanted to be a Pastor when she got older. The children would tease her because she was a disabled child but very intelligent. They would mess with her and call her names. That day, Maxine got mad, and she started chasing them and they all were scared, screaming and running. It wasn't Mary and her sisters that were teasing her, but they were in the crowd and start running too. Wanda and Wendy are Mary's sisters. Wanda fell down and hurt herself, and she was calling everyone to help her. Some of the kids stopped and the rest kept running; they looked back and were like, "OMG! Maxine picked Wanda up and threw her down hard on the ground." The kids tried to help, by throwing things at Maxine. Maxine was trying her best to get another victim, wanting to even the score for messing with her. Someone came along and made the children stop. But Wanda had a black eye, the next day; it was funny and it wasn't because that girl could have done even more damage than just that. Yet that is what a person gets when you bully another person and they never did anything to you. The kids also used to mess with old lady Gertrude. They loved playing in the woods, throwing little rocks at that lady. Mrs. Gertrude would chase them with that cane and they ran fast! They were out of breath by the time they got home. But those was the breaks" break it up, break it up, break down. Never bully, it is not good because some children are taking their own lives and it shouldn't be that way. Everyone wants to be love and wants attention.

Be careful of who you talk about and who you mess with. You never know how your children might turn out and who may bully you. Be friendly with everyone because you don't know what people are going through at home or school, etc. That person might be the one who has to save you one day. Maxine was one person who had to help some of the kids that picked on her and they all love her now. God can indeed make your enemy your footstool. Just by showing love to all can change people's lives. Never let anyone control you or block your view. Stop bullying, stop talking about people and learn to show love. They used to say, back in the old days" if you don't have anything good to say, don't say nothing at all. Or, "don't let one monkey stop the show" or your vision. This could have stopped Maxine from her goals or dreams. Be nice to others and never bully people.

Mary's mother never told them to hate people because of their color. Never allow the color of a person's skin stop you from a goal or dream. Shelly believed in Martin Luther King, Junior's speech and dream. For all to love and have peace; all over the world. It doesn't matter, we all live in this world together and on this earth. We all came into this world alone and are leaving alone (1 Timothy 6:7). Shelly raised her children well and taught them how to be respectful to everyone. Remember, I've got nothing but love for you, baby! I've got nothing but love for you, baby! Love everyone, all the world needs is love. Mary used to like a young man named Jimmy; he had medium brown skin and was bow legged. He was older than she was but Mary had a crush on him and he liked her. She liked his smile and his walk. It was a hot day, and school was over. Jimmy had his shirt off and his pants were hanging down some. He was walking past Mary's house. There were a few girls and boys outside playing marbles. It looked like Jimmy didn't have on any underwear, so they made up this song about him. Mary really didn't like it. The song was, "Jimmy went to school butt naked, butt naked, Jimmy went to school butt naked all through the town." They were playing with him but he didn't get mad. Jimmy just laughed at them. He was a good-hearted person. Mary thought he was a cute brown skinned young man. Remember the song, "I got a crush on you," by Lil Kim. He was a "mind blowing decision," a head on collision, but he was just a friend and he was just her friend. Jimmy had a vision to marry Mary when they got older.

Look back over some of your past good memories, compared to the world surrounding us today. It's just not the same anymore, but it's like that and that's the way it is. Don't let what's happening in the world distract your mind and your view of thinking big. Sing to yourself, "I got my mind made up, I can do what I want, anytime, today is fine." Life is what you make of it. You just have to keep on pushing, pushing it really good and move everything out of the way. You can blow people's minds with the things that you do and telling the world what you do. We need motivated people with big dreams and positive messages. They want you to tell them something good, tell them that you love them, yeah. Tell them something good. Tell them, tell them. Jimmy might have been Mary's man one day but Mary and her family had moved a year later.

It was nice living in the country, as long as there were no bats flying around in the house. Mary's mother would always straighten cousin, Aunt Irene's hair. Aunt Irene would already be drunk when she came to the house and still drinking. She always talked trash about some of the men, who she always argued with. Irene was a big lady about 300 pounds and loved to drink and fight. Ms. Shelly would straighten Irene's hair and she would start falling asleep in the chair, just snoring and she would always fall out of the chair! Mary would sit there, look at her and just laugh. Irene's head would be going sideways, backward and forward. She got burnt by the straightening comb a few times because she couldn't keep her head still. Madea said, "peace be still," and when someone is using a hot comb on your hair, be still. Aunt Irene didn't take no stuff off of men. She was a funny lady, who kept everyone laughing.

The children made their candy money by picking pecan nuts off the trees or off the ground, finding empty soda bottles and putting them in a big trash bag, next they put it in the wagon and would take it to the store for money. Remember the red wagon, that was the kid's transportation and Mary had a ball with it. She would hold the handle and someone would push her down the hill and you had to guide/steer the handle. They used to make their little coins instead of killing and robbing each other. Candy used to be a penny or five cents, and there was all kind of good candy. Remember the cherry clan candy, red hots, vintage candy, jolly rancher sticks, jaw breaker, squirrel nut zippers, bb bats candy, goobers box, bubblegum cigars, candy dish, lifesavers, lemon heads, hot jaw breakers, Boston baked beans, Clark bar, bazooka bubble gum, circus peanuts, candy necklace, kits, candy apples, now & later, candy dots, barrel candy, charm pops, pixie stick, Astro pops, juice in wax bottles, Mary Jane, etc. That candy was so good, even the church candy the kids got on Sunday mornings. The world was much better in the old days.

It was a Saturday evening, and all the kids decided to go in the woods. There was an old abandoned green house, and no one lived there for years. The door was unlocked and all eight kids went in the house. Someone had told the children an old man had lived there but he passed away. There was a rumor going around town that he kept a lot of money in the green house. Some of the children were looking for money, they went in one bedroom and it had spider webs everywhere. The second bedroom, one of the windows was broken and it had a bed with plenty of dust on it. The third room had a sign on the door that said, "do not enter," but the kids were running through the house and ran inside the third room. There was a big hole in the floor and half of Tony's body fell in the hole in that third room. The children didn't know what to do, they were frightened. They tried to pull him up but the floor was squeaking and felt like it wanted to cave in. One of the kids opened the closet door and Denise's foot got caught in a hole. They were so panicked and had no clue how to get out of this mess. Some were still trying to pull Tony out and others were trying to help Denise get her feet out. There was a man that lived in back of the house, he walked up to the house and asked, "Is anyone in here?" The kids were quiet, one child peeked out the window and saw the huge man, who was dressed up as a big bear because Halloween was in two days.

They were really scared and regretted that they went in the house. The man went outside and walked to the corner. The kids hurried up and pulled Tony up and got Denise out; they both were hurt. Once they got out of the house the man was walking back down. He saw the kids leaving the house and started chasing them. They were so scared, one of the kids fell down and three others fell on top of them. They feared for their lives and the man was almost upon them. The others kids kept saying, "get up; come on, he's getting closer!" They got up and ran like never before, the two kids that fell in the holes, you would have never known they fell because that is how frightened they were. The man dressed up in the bear suit was unable to catch the children. They ran so fast, it was like a storm that blew them away. They were serious now, no more laughing. They got home, removed their clothes, took a bath and said a prayer. They all talked about it over the next few days and laughed about how scared they were and it was fun because they got away. In the country, you had to do something to have fun and that is what the kids did -- instead of shooting and killing each other. These children had fun in their younger days but many kids today don't; and their vision is unclear to what path to take.

A fire broke out in the woods. It was a Friday, about 7 p.m. A few of the boys and girls got together and wanted to play the boys chase the girls. They were playing in the woods and decided to camp out. They got some sticks and wood to start a fire. A couple of boys had matches, so they lit the sticks and wood. It started burning and they all sat there talking, and just knew they were camping out. A few other kids had come along and started putting paper and other stuff on the fire. That made the fire get out of control and it started to burn some of the small trees near it. The woods caught on fire and the kids ran away. The children were always running but Ms. Hub saw Tony and told his parents. Tony had to tell on the other boys and girls that were with them. They all got in trouble, and were punished for three days.

There were some drugs users, weed smokers and plenty of drinkers. Mary didn't hear about too much killing and didn't see a lot of killing. She was small anyway but kids are smart and they learn fast. Mary while growing up had seen her mother and her mother boyfriend having an argument a few times and it hurt her to her heart. Her and her other brother and sisters were scared to go to school, because they were hoping and praying that their mom would be ok. Children hate seeing another person hurt and crying, it makes them cry too because they can sense something is wrong. Try not to fight or argue in front of your kids because they have feelings as well, it does not matter how small they are. They remember these things for a lifetime. Most children want their parents to get along. Even if you can't stand that man/woman, let the kids at least see you being friendly to each other and not arguing. Mary and her siblings went to church so God would help watch over their mom and them. And they all got out of that mess before things got too bad off. Tom could have seriously hurt Ms. Shelly, killed her or hospitalized her. Tom never hit Ms. Shelly but it looked like he wanted to. There are men who like to beat women and next thing you know, they want to make love to you. Make up, then you break up, that is a game for fools. First you love them; then you hate them, that's the games we play. Games people play.

There are some women who love to break up a happy home; they enjoy married men better and they know they can't always be around them. Some married men only see the ladies at the woman's home and never take them out in public because someone will see them. You never know who is watching. Tom was messing around on Ms. Shelly but she got fed up with the arguing and cheating. Sometimes you think your mind is playing tricks on you. All you can think of after being hurt, lied to and cheated on is, "I've got to leave," but your mind is telling you, "I just love that man, I don't care what you say; I just love him, I love him and I love him." But it takes a fool to learn that love don't love nobody. Being cheated on can hold people back from their vision or dreams. We have to learn to love ourselves first and have control over your thinking. Everything begins when we think and that thinking can be good or bad. Please be careful of your thoughts because it can cause your life to slip into a downfall. Minds are a terrible thing to waste. You have to let a man or woman know up front that there will be no half stepping. They are either so into you that they don't know what they are going to do, or else forget, there will be no relationship. Let them know to make up their mind and make that move right now, baby, because you only come around once in a lifetime. This world is full of games people play, games people play and are you down with opp. As Mary got older, she heard the song; you down with OPP; but she never knew what they were talking about until a young lady told her. Mary would just sing the song and had no clue what she was singing.

How many women have had men come up to them and say, "I want to know your name! I want to know your name." Then you get the relationship going on; the next the man asked, "can I take you out"; after that it's, "can I take you home," and "baby, I know you wondering if I can go over to your place." But they are not too sure about how the lady feels, so they rather go at her own pace. They (the men) wonder if they take you home, would you make sweet love tonight. The men have it planned out, and already know what they want. Once they get you, all they think about is; "me and Miss, Miss Jones, Miss Jones, Miss Jones, we got a thing going on." They tell you, "I'll be there, I'll be there: just call my name and I'll be there." You are calling his name, worrying where he is at and he is nowhere to be found. Mary's mother was a nice lady, just like many other women all over the world. We all were searching for true love and a good friend. But each time our heart got taken advantage of, it destroyed the dreams. We were looking for another person to complete us or make us whole; but only God can bring about true change in a human being.

Some women can't focus on their goals because they refuse to let go of that no good man who treated them wrong. No one can treat you or do you the way Jesus Christ can. He is the way, the truth and the life which gives us real life. Through it all, the pain, stress and letdowns; it never stopped Mary's mom from taking care of her kids and herself. She had a plan to move forward. Through it all, you learn to trust in Jesus; through it all, she learned to trust in God and she learned to depend upon His name. It just made her stronger and a little mean, when men would try to play games on her. She kicked their butt right out of her house and told them what they can do. Don't let people continue to hurt you, get out and stay focused. Women, sometimes you've got to give him up! No more crying but stand strong. Keep on dancing and moving on because you have to give him up.

Ms. Shelly liked the song, "she used to be my girl, I respect her, when she was mine, I never neglect her, she used to be my girl." After that break up, Shelly began partying to, "Got to give it up, I used go out and party; and shake it down." She had got herself together now and she felt alright. Tom on the other hand was singing, "Girl, I been missing you, the way you made me feel inside, what can I do? Come to me, baby; let me ease your mind and I can give you all the loving you need." Tom said, holding back those years of time that he will keep holding on. Shelly, however, would not take Tom back and there was no way he could ease her mind. He could only keep holding on and dreaming. Because there would be no more of them together. Shelly is a very special lady, and we all are special ladies, sitting on top of the world. Shelly twisted and turned until she got away from Tom. She told herself, "I got to be strong, he did me wrong, and she wasn't going to be with him for long. She knew she loved him and he wanted her. Tom said he wanted her but he knew he did her wrong. He asked Shelly, why can't we be friends, why can't we be friends? Shelly let him know it's all over and she didn't want him anymore. She said, "I don't love you anymore, it just that simple." Tom was able to see his twins and was forgiven for all his wrongdoing. He also apologized and said he was very sorry for arguing over nothing and making Ms. Shelly upset.

Always remember, forgiveness is for the person who is hurting and is miserable because they feel that someone has done them wrong. It also can help the person who caused you pain too. It can change the lives of both people. Always forgive out of the kindness of your heart. Once they let go of the pain, forgive the person, they will feel relief and peace will flow through the body. You will think better, feel better, have more energy and move into victory. Which makes your vision clear and your mind can progress much better.

The relationship ended. Tom just kept singing, "Missing you is all I keep dreaming of; kissing you is all I keep dreaming of!" Shelly was singing, "If I had one wish and wishes came true; I wish I could find a man of my dreams." Shelly waited patiently; she knew one day she would have that man of her dreams. She danced around her home and was singing, "I got to find me a man, I don't care what you say; I got to find me a man; to treat me the way that I want to be treated when I need to be loved. There is nothing like the real thing, baby, there is nothing like the real thing. Those sweet memories, I know you can see them now; those sweet memories I have tweeted them out my mind.

Sexy love, you had me crawling back to you but now I see what my beauty means to me."

Realize your brokenness; know that you need to change and move on. Mary loved her mom and liked the way she handled circumstances in her life, as well as taking very good care of all her children. Shelly's vision helped her stay focused on what she needed to continue to do in order to keep her body in good shape and her mind sharp.

# Mary's Family Moves

◇◇◇◇◇◇◇◇◇◇◇◇◇◇◇◇◇◇◇◇◇◇◇◇◇

Mary and her mother (Shelly) were so glad they moved. It was time for a new change and better life. A new mindset and some important decisions to be made. They ended up staying with Ms. Shelly's best friend, whose name was Maria. She was a single lady with no children. She was very kind and had a nice big house with a spacious yard, four bedrooms, three bathrooms, a big basement and lots of space. She owned her own business, had her investments set up for retirement, and she had a saving account and a coach. The kids didn't have to be apart from their mom but Ms. Shelly had to get on her feet. She had to find a job and she did. Her girlfriend (Maria) had to show Shelly around town. Shelly learned fast. She had money saved for twelve months of living expenses. She was able to do so because Tom had paid all the of bills when they were living together. That was a smart move, since instead of spending all her money she saved it for an emergency. If Shelly didn't learn anything else, her vision was clear enough to save money. She started working and they moved about one year later. Maria told them that they could have stayed as long as they liked. She let Shelly save her money because she was a millionaire. She wanted to make sure Shelly had a good amount of money before she left her home, and for her part Shelly didn't want to invade on her friend's private life. Shelly and her children thanked Maria very much for letting them stay with her. Maria told her no problem, she really enjoyed their company and the children gave her no problem. Maria told Shelly if she ever needed her, please let her know. The two women are best friends and are like sisters.

Mary and her siblings had to get up early in the morning while it was still dark. They went across the street to a neighbor's house who had her own daycare. She was a brown skinned, slim lady, very nice, she had one son, and always kept her house neat and clean. In one of the rooms, there was stuff everywhere, her son's toys, games, bike and other riding toys. The children always played in that room before they went to school. Mary and the other kids liked going over there. Mary's mother had to be at work real early, about 6 a.m. They all had, to stay there until it was time to go to school. Mary would go to the store and always buy an onion pickle; most of the school kids would go to the store for their snacks. The store opened early and it was packed. You could walk to school and in your neighborhood without getting shot. Many children are getting shot nowadays and they are getting younger and younger. Mary's mother, Ms. Shelly worked all her life. She knew how to budget her money and took good care of herself and her kids. Mary went to church with her mother's girlfriend and enjoyed going but all the other children fell asleep in church. They didn't like going all the time but Mary didn't mind because she always went to church before they moved.

It is important to forgive and have your priorities in order. Do you see how Mary's mother forgave Tom and had money saved to find a place? To pay the rent up, she had money to ride the bus and money to help pay bills. But her girlfriend didn't want any money from Shelly. Maria wanted Shelly to add to the savings that she already had, and to take her time to find a nice area and home for herself and her children. People never know what they might need money for and when things may fall apart or get out of control. Ms. Shelly always had her finances, life insurance and other family needs in order, for herself and for her children. Once the kids were grown, they took over their own life insurance policy and savings. Get your finances in order! We all need to be mindful and forever thankful for what you've got. No, we may not drive a great big car or have a nice sized house, but long as you are living, be thankful for what you do have. If you have to stroll back down memory lane and look things over, do that. Shelly got a place of her own a year later and the children loved their new house. It was a nice row house, four bedrooms, two full baths and a basement. Mary's mother kept, her house neat and clean as always.

The kids met new friends, went to a new school and the neighborhood had friendly people. Mary met a girl named Betty; she was older than Mary but couldn't come outside of her backyard gate. Betty would always call Mary to her gate and talk to her. Betty was adopted and they would not let her come outside those gates. All Betty could do was look at all the other kids having fun, running up and down the alley. Once Betty got older she was fast and a hot little girl. She had about seven kids. She also ended up on drugs and had some of her kids taken away from her. She was a nice person but not being able to play and interact with other children caused her to run wild and enjoy herself after she finished school and got up in age enough to move out. But she also ran with the wrong crowd and messed around with all the wrong men. Mary never saw her again, once they had moved but people had told her how Betty was doing and it was not good. Give your kids a little space because it might affect them in the long run. You can sit outside and watch them play, after you get your housework done. And the children do their chores. Let the children play as long as everyone is playing nicely. These days you should keep an eye on them anyway, it's more dangerous now. Shelly always watched her kids, took them to the park, took them shopping and sat outside while the children played around.

Mary got bullied a few times by one of her neighbors who lived around the corner. The girl just kept kicking her chair, almost every day in Spanish class. Mary asked the teacher to move her but the girl would still find a way to sit in back of her. Mary wasn't a person who liked to fight, she just wanted to get her education and get out of school. Mary was in middle school at the time. The girl was one of a set of triplets and they all liked Mary's brother but this girl was more like a tom boy. The cutest triplet out of the three was trying to get with Mary's brother, but he didn't care for any of them. Maybe that was why the young girl was kicking Mary's chair. It's hard to figure why the teacher didn't see this, as they were directly in front of the blackboard, right in the first row, very close to the teacher's desk. The teacher finally did something about it, but Mary was so ma she went home and told her brother. A lot of her brother's friends didn't know he had sisters because he was always by himself. But Mary was one of his favorite sisters and they both had the same dad. Once she told him, he waited until school was over and as they got close to the house at the parking lot, he beat up all three triplets up and their oldest sister, too. Her brother Sly could fight; he tore their tails up, and Mary had no more problems after that. He told her, don't ever wait a long time to tell him and to let him know right away. They had two brothers but they didn't come help the girls out and Sly wasn't scared anyway, he told them to go get them. Nobody else messed with Mary, her sisters or their mother.

Mary's brother Sly had plenty of lady friends. They all liked Mary, but she knew her brother was doing these girls wrong. Mary tried to tell one of the women what her brother was doing and that he was cheating on her. She was a good lady, worked, didn't take no stuff and was very smart. She really loved Sly and was always there for him when he needed her. But he was that sweet talker, dressed well and would always touch these girls' bodies and they liked it. A few of Mary and her sisters' friends would come see them and Sly would get fresh with them. Not all of Mary's girlfriends, however, because she had some nice friends and they didn't let anyone treat them wrong. They carried themselves very well. But many of the girls liked her brother. Some of the girls were even sisters, some lived next door (neighbors), others lived around the corner and all over town. Sly had girls everywhere he went. This man was well known and also stayed in trouble. Later he was in and out of jail. You can say he was a one-man army like Sylvester Stallone. He was smart, cool and got along with many people. The women took care of him. They just loved that man! They didn't care what he did, they just loved him, loved him and loved him. They would do anything for Sly, buy him clothes, brought him drugs in jail and money. Whatever he wanted he got it.

With some of the females, he would take over one of his other lady friend's houses and they all would sleep in the girl's mother's house in the basement, all in the same bed together. You can say, they just loved that man and they didn't care what you say; they just love him, they love him and love him. "They treated him so good and they just loved him. It takes a fool to learn that, love don't love nobody." The women loved the pleasure of being with this man. Their focus was on the wrong things and it was having fun and feeling good. And it's not much different in the world today. Their focus was on, "I want to sex you up!" The ladies would tell Sly," I'm not asking for too much just a, little of your time;

just a couple of forever; I'm the only one and you are the only one I need. "All these ladies were crazy in love. Sly was smooth. Most of these women ended up on drugs because of the fast lifestyle, the stealing and the drugs. He didn't care how many women he was messing with, they were happy when he was with them. When they were with him, they made sure they had a good time. When they would see him, it was like Christmas, Thanksgiving or Happy New Year for them. What a shame. He kept their minds burning and it kept them confused. Anyone who had a heart would love these women, the same way they loved Sly. They treated him like a King. Anyone who had a heart wouldn't hurt these women, lie to them and be untrue, knowing that these women love you so! Anyone with a heart would take them and love them too. Time was passing them all by, without any of them realizing, their why. Why am I putting up with this nonsense?

Sly loved all the women of the world. They loved for him to ring their bell. "You can ring my bell, al, al ring my bell." He was definitely ringing some bells. And the ladies were putting on their mommy boogie shoe. They would say, "I want to put on, my mommy, mommy boogie shoe." They would go out and party, dancing all across the floor. "Hey, let's do it, let dance, let's dance across the floor; hey, let's do it, let's dance, let's do it some more!"

One lady got into an argument with him because he lied about having a lady. She found out that he was someone else's guy, the first day of September, after all that bull he put her through. Then she found that he was someone else's lover. So, those boogie nights were all over with her. Sly told her, if loving you is wrong, he didn't want to do right; he didn't want to do right because she meant so much to him. She told him to leave and the beat goes on, and the beat goes on. Sly said, "But I got nothing but love for you, baby, I got nothing but love for you." This lady was named Kathy, she had a nice personality, was a little on the heavy side but was sweet as can be and sweeter than pie. She told Sly, "You will not bump no more with this big fat woman, you will not bump no more with this big fat woman, you done hurt my heart and have let me down, you done let me down." Kathy told him, all these years we put in the relationship, I just wanted to get married, I just wanted to get married. And making love to anyone was just not going to work. Kathy told Sly, "You made my heart beat, but now you made my heart feel so weak and you made me feel weak at the knees. Those sweet memories are dead and gone." Sly walked away and it was another one bites the dust another one bites the dust and he moved on to the next in line. He never dreamed or had any kind of goals whatsoever.

There was, however, one main chick that Sly really did love and she loved him, but he wasn't faithful to her. She gave him everything too. She got caught up in that one-night love affair and was in love. Every time Sly would mess up, she would forgive him and take him back. Helen was back in love again. Sly loved her, he told her if this world was his, he would place at her feet all that he owned because she had been so good to him. If this world was his, oh baby he would give her anything. He would give her flowers, a ring, and his heart; if this world was his, he would give her anything! Helen told him, "You don't want to fix the problem, you don't want to break up," and she can't wait around for him.

Sly told Helen, "My heart is yelling for your love."

Helen told him, "You can't keep running in and out of my life. I've never felt this way before and your love has come into my heart. You are a good man but you always fall for all of Satan's treats, in the world."

Sly said, "No other love can light my life and no one can do the things you do to me or for me."

Helen said, "Why do you treat me so bad and why do you do me the way you do? All the things you should have said and all the things you should have done, I shouldn't be crying; make all this pain go away."

Sly said, "No one said it would be easy, sorry you had to put up with me, please stay, stay, stay with me, I want you to stay. I know I messed up and broke your heart but hearts can heal."

They separated for some months to really see what was out there in the streets and test the waters. Sly said, "I miss you and I am not single but when I see you in the streets, I am going to speak."

Helen told Sly, "You took my love for granted, you will miss me when I am gone. My love will stand tall as a tree, spread wide as the sea, and shine bright as the stars as a night; our love will always be together."

Sly told Helen, "I do love you, I love you, I love you and oh, every man deserves a good woman and I just want to let you know how much I need you. Don't you know I will get down on my knees for you, baby. I can never love no other, when we are not close to one another; I just want you so bad. You gave me good love."

Helen told Sly, "You need to learn to appreciate me because my days are cold without you and my heart can't take no more. When you left me, I lost a part of me!"

Sly said, "Can you stand the rain, no pressure, no pressure from me, baby. I need you; I want you and I love you. All I need is a shoulder to cry on, I want to be down, I want to be down with you."

Helen told Sly, "Do you know how sweet and wonderful life can be? If you don't want me, let's just kiss and say good bye forever."

Sly told Helen, "The closer I get to you, the more you make me feel; by giving me all your love, your love has made me free. I will be a better man; look out, baby, because here I come. There ain't no woman like the one I got, she makes me happy, so very happy, this I can bet because she stood right beside me and I was so glad. I will not be foolish no more; you are my everything and I'll be around."

Helen said, "What do you do when you love somebody and everything starts falling apart? Oh, here we go again. Oh, here we go again, I thought what we had was over now. But here we go again; we keep coming back to each other."

Sly was a smooth, down to earth man but Helen was his main squeeze. She was the smartest woman out of all the women Sly fooled around with and she was very outspoken. Some guys better watch out, some girls are only about that thing or money. It takes a fool to learn that love don't love nobody. Sly had someone good and a true mate. You never miss the water until the well run dry.

She had a very good job and was pregnant with twins by him, but got rid of the babies because he told her to. This didn't stop her from her vision. She still was in her right mind; she didn't end up on drugs and she finally let go of Sly because he didn't treat her fairly. But it hurt her to her heart because she cared for him so much. We have to stay focused, keep your mind clear so you can see your vision/dreams come true. She did get married and had kids by another man but wasn't as happy as she was with Sly. She wished Sly could have changed his ways but he never did. She had to stop in the name of love. So, he wouldn't keep breaking her heart. She had to get over it. So many of us get caught up in these relationships, looking for love in all the wrong places and expect a person to fill all our needs but God is the answer to that kind of love. Relationships can stop your dreams from coming true and hinder a male or female's vision. Be strong and move on, we all deserve better. But seek God first and all these things would be added on to you. Mary and her brother were very close and she loved all her brothers and sisters. Sly had a good girl but was young and was blind. He had no sense of direction and the paths he took were not the correct way of a good life. He thought he was living his best life. Please be careful of the life that you choose because it can take you out of this world or make your life much better.

One day, one of the triple brothers got Sly back for beating up his sisters. He talked over a plan to rob some people at a mall and knew they wouldn't get much money. So, they robbed the people and the triplets' brother got caught and claimed that Sly was there too. The police went to Sly home, early in the morning about 4:00 a.m., and banged on the door, scaring his mother and the other kids, as everyone had been asleep. His mother answered the door and the police had big rifles out and pointed them at her. Some were at the back door making sure he didn't run. They said he was armed and dangerous. He was there and they locked him up. There are so many cops, it looked like something in the movies. He had just got out of jail a few months earlier and now back he went again. He had a history of being locked up, so if someone said his name the police knew who he was. Some people said, once you go to jail you always go back. He was a young man in and out of jail. One thing was for sure, he never snitched on anyone, he did his time and when he came out, he was right back with the same people. He had no goals, dreams or a vision to better himself. No dreams of getting married, having a family and being with a nice lady. The woman he had, he blew that chance and never found another love like that again. He was a street boy. No father role model and he would always hang around with the wrong guys. The life he lived was live or die. He never accepted Jesus Christ into his life and only went to church when he was a small child. Which at that time, a child never really understood who Jesus was! Sly only knew that his mother sent him to church. But he did take care of himself, could fight and wasn't scared of anything at all. He was funny, loving and many people loved him. He was a little gangster and took no mess off anyone.

Sly last lock up was when a bank robbery took place and his mother had to go find him. The police wanted him badly and his mother was so scared. The police threatened the mother and told her if she didn't go get him and bring him home, they were going to lock her up. She was so scared and crying. She wished her son didn't get in so much trouble but she did her best raising him. Ms. Shelly and one of her girlfriends went to pick him up. One of the car windows was broken, the driver's side of the car. Mary rode with them; she was so close to her brother and they all felt bad because he stayed in a mess. Riding up in her mother's girlfriend's car was a nightmare. When going to pick up Sly, her mother's girlfriend was driving off the road and the car was going out of control for some reason. The car wouldn't stop and they all were so frightened. But her mother's friend called on the name of Jesus a few times when she realized the car was about to go over the side of the mountain. Mary's mother's friend called on the name of Jesus so loudly, and the car stopped!

Jesus was with them that day, as always. You have to have faith as small as a mustard seed. Jesus is unbelievable. It was so cold because the window was out and her mom was scared and upset. Sly turned himself in and he won the case. Your mind is a terrible thing to waste, so think of something positive, help someone not do the things you do and tell them how your life change for the better. The road seems real dark, people fall down, get back up, fall again into that same hole and just can't stop falling into that same hole. Never finding a way out, but there is light at the end of that dark road. He never found his way out of darkness, which was Satan's kingdom. God gives us power and His word; we must use it in order to get out of bad situations. We fall down but we can get back up again, but you have to make that decision, to change and let go of some things, people, bad habits and places. Be that blessed man/woman (Psalms 1:1). You can only do it with God's help. God's is so good and He loves us all. Show love and respect for one another and stop hurting each other. Life is so short. Do you see how the months are just flying by? We are running out of time. Get a vision and see what God has for you.

Mary's mother's house was where the party would be. They had house parties all the time and also in the back yard. They were having a house back yard party; I mean back yard house party. Everyone was getting down. "Get down, get down! Get down, get down and the party was jumping. Jump, jump, jump to it, jump, jump, jump, to it, to it." They would dance to express yourself, believe, express yourself, believe, express.... believe. Songs they used to jam to: "Freak out, freak out, hey, let's dance, let's dance, let's dance across the floor, hey, let's do it, let's dance and let's do it some more." They danced to, "Let's whip, whip it, baby, whip it right, just whip it, whip it, baby, whip it all night." It was so much fun party, laughing, talking and joking around. They danced the night away. Mary liked one of Sly buddies, but they would just talk as friends. Sly didn't like for any of his friends to talk to his sisters. Remember Scarface? Sly probably would have hurt one of his friends over one of his sisters. Especially if they tried to mess over them. These guys, that is all they, did hung in the street and had girls all over the place. They all did good over the years, until they got ahold of some of the most powerful drugs. Many passed away from trying to sell drugs; next thing you know they were using it themselves. You can't sell drugs and use them. Because you will end up messing the people's money up and they will be after you. It is a hard life to live because it is about life or death, prison or freedom and like or hate. Sly was a cool man but needed a positive outlook on life. He needed a better crowd to hang with, but he was loved by many people. Have a goal/vision, so you don't have to watch over your back all the time and live with peace in your mind. These days now, you have to watch your back no matter what because of the changes in the world 2020 and years before. The Bible says many are called but few are chosen because they do not prepare themselves. Make a major decision in your life and be the best you can be.

# Mary's Life (Teenager/Adult)

◇◇◇◇◇◇◇◇◇◇◇◇◇◇◇◇◇◇◇◇◇◇◇

Growing up in the city was nice at first, back in the 1970s. You could leave the doors unlocked. People would knock even though your door was open. Many children used to skate in the streets, ride their bikes, hang out on the porch late night and talk. No one ever talked about money, investments, business or dreams; and it wasn't taught in school. School nights, Mary and her other siblings had to come in early. Their mom didn't play that, they were in the house once it got dark. They would hang out the window talking to friends. They also would play a game called, that is my car! When the cars would ride up and down the street. They would say, that's my car and whoever said it first it was their car. Nowadays the children are out late nights, looking to harm and damage things that people own. Their parents should be teaching them about a goal or make them read books. Most of them are very young, they are killing, stealing, raping women/girls and have no respect for anyone. There are small things you can do which are positive: like clean cars, be a helper in a store, find summer job cleaning the streets, sell frozen cups, make cupcakes, cut grass, and be respectful to everyone. But now you have to be careful of selling anything out of your homes due to Coronavirus disease. Mrs. Shelly used to make frozen cups, all different flavors and cupcakes. The people enjoy them and when Mary's mom ran out of something, she would let the people know when the frozen cups and cupcakes would be ready. Her mom also made some good sweet potato pies, they were delicious. Not everybody can make good pies. Women and men would ask her to make some pies for them and they paid for the pies. You can make money all kinds of ways. That is a small goal, vision or dream to get you started and make some money.

Mary's mom worked in the bakery, most of her life. Ms. Shelly could cook and bake. Shelly was a nice lady and loved all of her children. She never complained about raising them alone as a single mother. She went to work, never liked being late and when she wasn't feeling well, she still went to work. Unless she was really sick but that wasn't too often. Shelly took care of herself and the kids. Nothing held, her back from moving forward. As long as she had her children, that was one happy woman. Let no man/woman stop you from spending time with your children. You don't need money all the time to be with your children, it is the quality time you spend with them that makes all of the difference in their life: just as well as in your life, you spend time with your own mother/father. Even a phone call almost every day, will make a difference. Hearing a parent's voice is important to boys/girls. Love your kids, it also helps with the vision or road they are going to take for the future. Shelly's dream came true, she had her own Bakery and dependable workers. She treated them fairly and would pay them good.

Mary's first job was cleaning the streets and you had to be 15 or 16 years old. She brought her own school clothes and that made it easier on her mom. In high school, she worked at a restaurant with her mom. Most of the time you had to count on your tips to have good money. Many times, people wouldn't tip. Sometimes you would have a big group that tipped small. Sometimes there were one person who tipped well. It is the same today; waitresses make very little in tips and some might get a nice tip. Later she worked in a store, with clothes. She had a friend who worked there too. Kim was her name, this girl used to steal underwear sets for her boyfriend. Her boyfriend had all the color sets. He had the light and dark colors, in brown, blue, green, only black, purple, red, etc. Next, Kim started stealing jewelry and it was all real. Her boyfriend started wearing the jewelry and selling some of it and Kim never saw any of the money. She was mad because she almost got locked up for stealing all the merchandise. People were warning them to stop stealing because the manager started realizing that items were missing. They would always count the items at the end of the day. Next a supervisor told everyone that someone was stealing and to stop. Kim didn't listen, so one day she was in the store and they told everyone in there to go form a line on the side of the wall and they started patting them down. Kim was like, I don't have anything but they did find a ring on her. Kim stopped them and said, I don't have anything else and told them not to touch her.

They took Kim in their office and started questioning her. She was a very quiet young lady and everyone was so surprised that she was one of the people stealing. Kim was loaded with items on her but they didn't touch her again because they couldn't believe she would do such a thing. They asked her where did she find the ring and she said she saw it laying there so she picked it up. They asked she saw anyone stealing and she said no. They believed her but she was out of a job. If they would have continued patting her down, she would have been in jail. God was with her that day because she had stolen so much stuff from them. When they let her go, Kim had to wait on the bus right across the street from her job. She thought the security was watching her but they were making sure she left the job site. When that bus came, she got on there so fast, and kept praying and hoping they weren't following her home. When she got to her home, she was looking around and praying no one was behind her. Because she had plenty of stolen goods in the house, plus on her but they didn't follow her. She was so scared but no one suspected that she would do something like that. Kim got away with it for a while and never went back that way again. After that she would ask her mom for a few dollars until she got another job. Kim got another job in two weeks. She worked at that job for six months and the police came to her mom's home to arrest Kim. They had found out she was the thief and she got two years in prison because she never did anything before. Kim had a clean record, until someone told her to steal from that old job. It could have cost her, her life in jail or a long sentence. She was blessed and highly favored, nothing but God. Kim learned from her mistake; she asked God to forgive her. She now has a men's clothing store.

Mary and her other siblings would comb their mom's hair after work and help her with her feet. Shelly was able to give them money, when the kids asked for it. She was making good money. Nowadays children want way more money than what their parents can afford and the parents don't have money to throw away. Men/Women are barely paying their rent and are able to buy food. Be thankful for what you've got, thank God for every day you are living and have breath in your body. When Mary attended school, it wasn't as bad as it is today. There were no cell phones, no beepers, people had house phones, no computers, we had books to read, and no Facebook drama. We remembered friends and family's phone numbers by heart or had it written down somewhere. Many people today don't have to remember people's phone numbers because it is in their cell phones. Many refuse to wear watches anymore because they can tell time on their cell phone. We need to keep all phone numbers in a telephone book, in case something happens to your phones. Keep the mind sharp, we used to remember people's phone number by heart. You could walk the streets at night and sleep better without hearing gunshots every other night.

Children walked to school, some caught the MTA bus and some rode the school bus if they lived way across town. The children years ago walked to school in the snow, rain, hailing and bad weather. Nowadays, if you have bad weather conditions they close school for almost anything. The family always had fun together, laughed, played ball, had cookouts, cried together, talked and played cards. Today Mary's family still have plenty of fun and travel together. The women in the family talk about relationships and many other topics. The women just laugh and try to support each other by giving positive feedback on the situation. There are males and females who are afraid to be alone and feel empty because others have someone by their sides. Believe it or not, it is good to be alone for a period of time. Always take time out for yourself, God and your children. Get a vision, not on a man/woman you want but what do you want to happen in your life. Is that what's been holding many of us back, a bad relationship/marriage? Think about you right now and how you would want your life to be like.

Mary had a few bad experiences with relationships. Her first love was the one she truly loved and just knew it would last forever. She had no clue that it would end one day. He wished for Mary on a falling star and they ended up in a relationship. They were like best friends and did everything together. They were always together most of the time and very happy. Mary's mother Shelly liked Moe; he was nice built, pretty smile, respectful and a gentleman. They went walking, watched movie together, drank beer together, played ball, had cookouts and went to some house parties together. They would go over a couple of his friend apartment/place and hang out. When you saw Moe, Mary was somewhere near him. As time went on people started wanting her man and he started smelling himself. He decided to play games like everybody else and some of his buddies. He would act like he was at one of his friend's places and Mary would go look for him. Most of the time he was not there. Mary knew something was wrong because they were always together most of the time and if she couldn't find him, he was out doing another chick. His friends would answer the door and say they hadn't seen him. Sometimes he wouldn't come straight home from work and stay out all night. When she did catch up with Moe, he had an excuse for where he had been. Next, they would be together for a while and he would escape again. Mary would be hot, pissed off and went looking for him all night. A few times she found him over some lady's house and she would knock on the door and Moe would come out. Moe would get his belongings and leave with Mary. They would argue, be mad with each other for days then get back together. Later Moe repeated the same mess all over again.

Moe's house phone rang a few times and Mary would answer the phone and it would be a girl calling for Moe. Mary and the girl on the phone would start arguing. When Moe came downstairs in the basement from taking a shower, him and Mary were arguing. Everything wasn't peaches and cream anymore, because Moe was following his friend's footsteps and Mary decided to play too. Mary started having her guy friends on the side. When she couldn't find Moe, she called one of her male friends and went to spend time with them. They both got caught a few times with other people. But they still stayed together and wanted to make it last forever. Mary knew she would have to give him up because the pain it was causing her was not a good feeling. She didn't want to have to keep chasing after Moe, looking for him, going crazy over him and crying all day and night. Women/Men never chase after a person who you are in love with and you think they love you. If they love you, you shouldn't have to search for them. They should love you, like you love them. Treat you the way they want to be treated. Having you upset and worried is not love.

Mary could have ended up on drugs or anything. She did her own investigating. When you find out the truth, you have a choice to stay in the relationship or get out of it. If you know he is seeing other women, it's no need to look for him again because if you can't find him; you already know he is with someone else. Especially when you haven't talked to him in days and he hasn't been home for days. This can also mess up your eyesight and range of view, for your vision. Men can tell you lies and try to make it sound so good. Make sure you listen to everything they say, every word that proceeds out of their mouths because sometimes things just don't add up right. They will also try to change the subject, once you know they are lying. Pay attention to the details your man may give you. They can drive you insane and no you don't want to keep running after them and trying to find them. Mary was focused on the wrong things and she couldn't see the good that was in front of her.

There is no reason for you to keeping hurting and being stressed over a man that treats you with no respect. First, they love you, then they hate you; that is a game for fools. Break up then make up; those are games that people play a lot. These games can mess up a person's thinking and their vision to success. Live your life, live your life and take your time and be single. You don't need to sleep with every Dick and Harry. Let them chase you and still take your time. It is better to be safe than sorry, happy than weak, have a clear mind than a cloudy mind, and a brain that can think for itself instead of being brainwashed. Who wants a man/woman that lies all the time? Once you tell one lie, you have to keep telling lies. Next you run out of lies and start getting caught in them. Have you ever heard of a man's phone always off, not charge, claiming they didn't know where they put their phone, it'd be off for days, you can't get through but other people call him and he answer. Or when you call from a different number; they will pick up the phone. He could have more than one phone but you don't know, and when he is ready to talk to you; he turns it on and tells you the same lies as always. They know who they can lie to and get away with it and you believe them; after you cried all night and went looking for them; they were nowhere in town to be found. Later they tell you, they were out of town. If he truly cared about your feelings, he would have called and gave you some heads up with what was going on and what his next move would be. Women, why did he not call you, if he truly love you?

She shouldn't be crying over you, all day and all night. Put yourself in her shoes. Women, we have to be strong and learn to love God the way we love these men. If there was no sex involved, I wonder, what will happen and will you still be so in love. Is it the sex thing, that makes everyone lose their minds, and block your view? You never want to give that man/woman up but people don't know how to fully love one another. Are you a fool in love? After Moe had a child by another woman, Mary stayed a little longer in the relationship because she loved him very much. She knew it would be time to leave and start a new life alone without Moe. That really hurt her soul and she just couldn't believe the man that wished for her on a falling star and said he loved her, would do something like that to her. Mary was weak and in so much pain. That was her true sign from the Lord to move. Mary left Moe; she didn't want to, that was her other half and he had the key to her heart but the key got lost. It was a disaster, a loss to Mary but she had to leave him. Moe began going downhill, ended up on drugs and drinking heavily. He had white lines going through his mind and up his nose. He started seeing all kinds of women who were using drugs and having sex with three and more people.

People were telling Mary that Moe was getting into fights for running her mouth and being high. It's sad to see a person get caught up and running with the wrong crowd. He told people after his break up with Mary, that she was the only woman he truly loved and was going to marry her someday. Mary had moved on and was in another relationship years later. She didn't rush into the relationship because Moe was her first lover and she deeply cared for and loved him from the bottom of her heart. He was a friend, a friend of Mary's, the one she thought was true to her but out of all the love in the world, she believed he was the one. But he broke her heart and the trust was gone because of Moe. The man that meant so much to her. She loved Moe, it was nothing like the real thing, nothing like the real thing, baby; it was true love. But life goes on, the beat goes on and the beat goes on; time keeps on ticking, ticking, ticking into the future and her dreams are still with her. If only Moe would have stayed faithful to Mary. Maybe things would have been better for Moe. Love the one you are with and understand we all are valuable. You never know when a person will leave this earth. Please know that our Bible is our Basic Instruction Before Leaving this Earth.

Mary now had a real friend, true friend, faithful friend, true love, a friend to the end and a friend she can trust with all her heart. A friend, a friend, a friend like mine and yours; out of all the love in the world; Jesus is the one friend, who truly love her more. Proverbs 18:24, a friend who sticks closer than a brother. Proverbs 17:17, a friend loves all the time. Mary is a friend of God, James 2:23. She had to believe in Jesus Christ and trust the words in the Bible. This is what helped Mary through the good and bad days. Are you a friend of God? Are you a friend of God? Because He called Mary a friend of His. Avoid being afraid to break those chains off of you; in those bad relationship! Stop making excuses for a person who is not treating you the way you should be treated. When you need to be treated, in a loving way. Jesus can love you, take care of you and provide for you. He's alright, He's on time, He can turn your life around, He will give you a testimony and lift you up high. Don't run from fear but find the solution to all your problems. Then you can move on to bigger and better things; for yourself and children, if you have children. (Numbers 23:19) God is not a man that should lie, nor a son of man, that he should change his mind. Does He speak and then not act? Does He promise and not fulfill? God can and will heal you, if you just believe. Things will get better with Jesus Christ.

Mary's second relationship was good and she has falling in love for a second time with Tim. He was in the Army and worked. Tim would walk past Mary's house while going to work every day. Mary would be standing on her porch, every day, just watching Tim as he walked down the street. She would just watch that man; he had her interest in him. Mary was taking her time because of her first relationship. She was chilling and guarding her heart. Mary started finding ways to keep her mind off of Moe. It had been over two years now without Moe in her life and he didn't know where she lived. She thanked God, she didn't have any kids by Moe because it would have been strings attached to her. She had no reason to see him anymore because she had no kids with him, that was a blessing! There will be a time, we all have to count our blessings and not be stressed out. Tim was walking by one Friday morning and Mary decided to pull him over. They talked, Mary asked where was he going and he said to work. Mary asked what time did he get off? Tim told her he got off at 4:30 p.m. and works Monday through Friday. Mary asked Tim when can they get together and maybe go out to eat or go to a movie? Tim said, next Friday evening! Mary gave him her address and phone number. When that Friday came, that evening they meet and went out to eat. Tim had a big smile on his face, and he gave Mary his address.

They became close and were boyfriend and girlfriend. A year later, Tim moved in with Mary at her girlfriend house for about six months. Then the two moved back with their parents until they both saved up enough money to move on their own. Tim came to visit Mary one Saturday at her mom's house and Moe came over also. Moe was with Mary's brother Sly. Moe didn't like seeing Mary with another man and Moe tried to start a fight with Tim. Moe still loved Mary and seeing that she was pregnant, Moe didn't like that because someone else had Mary's heart! Mary was pregnant by Tim and that hurt Moe to his heart. Remember, Moe had a child while him and Mary were together and that hurt Mary. What goes around, sometimes come back around; we may not know how a person will get what they dish out because it can come back in all kinds of shapes and forms. Be very careful how you treat people. It took Mary and Tim about six months until they got their own place.

Moe did call Mary at her mom's house and wanted her back. He was staying with one of his sisters and wanted Mary to come over. Mary went over there one day to visit Moe and he was high. Mary felt bad because she was pregnant and was with Tim now. Her and Moe started to kiss but it just didn't feel right and Moe could not please her anymore. Mary had left, but talked to Moe only a couple more times on the phone. One day Moe called Mary and she wasn't home yet at her mom's house. Mary called him back later and some girl answered the phone and they got into an argument. After that Mary stopped returning his calls and she knew it was wrong anyway because she was with Tim and he was a good man. Mary forgave Moe for disrespecting her and cheating. Moe asked Mary why can't we be friends, why can't we be friends and she told him they can be friends. She still cared a little for Moe, because she was truly in love with him. Mary had moved on with her life and didn't want to hurt Tim because she knew how it felt to be hurt by someone you truly care about. It was hard to let go of that man, all those tears she cried, all that pain inside; it just wasn't worth her time anymore.

Chasing after him in the middle of the night and she couldn't find him sometimes, sleepless nights, drinking herself to sleep, being hung over trying to heal the pain, in and out of love and thinking to yourself, why is he doing this to me? Mary always wondered if it isn't love for Moe, why did it hurt so bad and made her feel so bad inside? What about some of you, if it isn't love why does it hurt so bad and make you feel so bad inside? When a woman or man get the strength to break away from all their stress, releasing all that pain it feels good, the body feels better and a person feels heathy. Mary was able to think better and her body was rebuilding strength. God has to remove some things in our lives and open our eyes. (Isaiah 42:7) To open blind eyes and to get the poison out. It is like we are prisoners in bad relationships, in jail, locked up because they feed us these love words and imprison us with the love they give. Many times, the women don't know how to get out and stay away from their lovers. You must learn to love yourself first and dream big dreams.

Those who sit in darkness, usually take years to realize what is going on. Many women stay in difficult relationship because they refuse to be alone. About three months later, Moe had got shot. He had ended up using drugs very heavily. Mary was surprised to hear that Moe passed away. It hurt a little and she did go to Moe's parents' house and went to his funeral. But it is sad, how these drugs are killing people and how they end up on drugs. Many come from good homes, some raised by both parents, many were middle class people, many got introduced by a good friend, one hit and you are hooked; some just got caught up with the wrong people. Moe had a good woman (a mate), who was by his side and once she was gone, his life did a downfall. Men, keep your women if you know you have a virtuous woman; who you can make your wife. Her worth is far above rubies (Proverbs 31:10). There are plenty of men who mess up when they have a virtuous woman or wife. Most of the time you will never find another love like this again. Find out what area in your life needs to be changed and change it. Many people don't know how to change, refuse to change, don't want to change and don't think they need to change. Take a good look at yourself and how you are living! Is there something you see, that need change? Stop refusing but accept the fact that you really do need help. Mary continued to move on and love the one who she was with, Tim.

Tim and Mary had their first townhouse, finished basement and big backyard. Everything was going well and they had their first child. Tim loved to play music and enjoyed buying fish. He was a family man, went to work and came home. Mary never had a problem with Tim cheating, didn't have any suspicious of him fooling around, and was happy together for about six years. Mary dud believe Tim had started getting high because he was coming in late sometimes. His mood had changed but Mary never knew too much about the different drugs people was using. It was their child first birthday party and Tim didn't make it. Mary had talked to Tim and he said he was on his way. Mary went on with the party and was waiting to sing Happy Birthday. She tried calling Tim and got no answer; she started to worry. Mary started getting upset because she had no clue where Tim could be. Only God knew what was going on (Ecclesiastes 3:1-8) Everything has its time. To everything there is a season, a time for every purpose under heaven.

About an hour later, Mary got a phone call that Tim was in the hospital. He was in a serious car accident and ended up in intensive care. Mary went to the hospital and he was in a lot of pain. He had a nice car and it got totaled. It took a month before Tim came home and they stayed in the town home for about three more months. Because Mary, found out that Tim was using drugs. He had no more car, was on crutches and once he got out of the hospital; he went around the corner to a friend's house on his crutches to get whatever he was using. Mary just couldn't believe it. These drugs were just taking over people's lives and controlling their minds. Mary was terrified, this second relationship made her feel she was going around in circles. She realized Tim had tried something that was not good for the body, just like Moe had done. Mary was thinking what is going on in this world and how do people get on such a powerful drug? A substance that controls a person's mind, has them walking like they are dead (the walking dead) and them losing their minds. People run to these drugs, sometimes you will see packs of people together waiting on a tester. It is unbelievable, the things they do for these drugs. They don't care about anything but using drugs. How can they like a feeling that you won't remember and not knowing what you have done from day to day, month to month and year to year? It is sad, wake up, wake up; life is passing you by! Mary had learned that it is hard to get free from this kind of substance abuse. One day Tim left home in the morning, was gone all day and never came home. The next day, still no Tim and Mary hadn't heard from him. Later that evening, one of Tim's relative or friend broke into their home. They had kicked the basement door in and Mary had no idea what was going on. She did know that she and her baby son were in danger. Mary, went and found Tim, he was out of town and still didn't come home. He was still using and Mary gathered her things and went to her mom's house.

They both ended up with their parents again. Tim was waiting on his accident money anyway. Once he got that, he bought another nice car and got them another townhouse. Tim was still dropping a little in drugs but Mary really couldn't tell. She had an idea because of the guys he was hanging with and they would come to the house or he would go to their house. These were grown men that still lived with their mother. They didn't have any kind of vision but doing drugs. Plus, Mary knew some of them got high and so Tim was too. He was spending the settlement money. He did come home and never stayed away again. But one day, Tim made a U-turn, God sent an angel to him and help Tim get his life back on track. They had a little girl and Tim began going to church. That was a blessing, for Tim. He later got his life lined up with God and he was doing much better. Once he got his life together, he left Mary and the children. The children were small, about three and four when he left them. Mary didn't have a phone but still had the place to stay in. She had to use the older lady's phone (her neighbor) and the lady was a little upset because Tim had left Mary and the children without a phone.

Ms. Taylor was upset, knowing Tim had that nice car he had bought and yet couldn't make sure the phone was on in Mary's home, in case something happened to the kids. Ms. Taylor was disappointed in Tim. He moved back into his mother's house and stayed there. Tim said it was a sin to live together and not be married. Mary was very disappointed with Tim. She had stood by his side and never left him while he was doing drugs and she had given him another child. Mary was upset again, her heart was heavy, she cried and cried, and couldn't understand why this man walked out on her and her kids. Mary knew she had to be strong and raise her children alone and that is what she did. Mary did get to know Jesus Christ, the One Who brought her out of her first relationship. Mary was hurting for a while but knew she needed God and He was able to help pull her through this second relationship too. Mary is doing well and she took care of both of her children. Tim never came around to see the children after he left Mary. He passed away ten years later.

Mary met a gentleman named Bill at the Pocono mountains, where she was with two of her girlfriends. Bill had seen Mary at the market twice and both times he was trying to talk to her. Mary did say hello back to Bill and she told him she was in a relationship, but she wasn't in a relationship. She was just trying to guard her heart after the last two relationships. For some reason, she just kept running into Bill. The last time Mary and her two girlfriends were at a restaurant, getting ready to eat dinner. Bill was in there alone. He walked over to the table and asked if could he buy all of the ladies a drink? Mary said no thank you but her friends said, sure. Bill bought them all drinks and paid for their dinners. Bill asked Mary if he could take her out Saturday night and she finally said yes, I would like to. Bill came and picked Mary up and they had a nice time together. Bill said he had no kids and had never been married. Mary told him a little about her life and that she had two children. Bill said he liked her when he first laid eyes on her. (Proverbs 16:24) "Pleasant words are like a honeycomb. Sweetness to the soul and health to the bones." He always opened the car door for her, he talked polite and was kind.

Mary's heart felt good and she liked his style. The Bible tell us; A merry heart does good like medicine, but a broken spirit dries the bones (Proverbs 17:22). Bill and Mary have been seeing each other for two years now. Bill asked Mary if she wanted to get a place together and get married later? Mary said she would think about it and let him know. Bill told Mary, heaven must have sent her from above. He said, the closer he gets to Mary the more she makes him feel like giving all his love to her and no one else. Mary said, some people are made for each other, some people can love one another for life and how about us? Bill said, he would love for that to happen because he had been searching for the right kind of woman. That he was looking for a real love. Bill told Mary, could it be that he is falling in love with her? Mary stated that she is a faithful lady. Mr. Bill said, he will never keep a secret and he will never tell a lie. Mary told Bill she is easy like Sunday morning. As they laid down in the bed, Bill began to sing in between the sheets. They were so in love and she knocked him off of his feet. This is how people think, they want love, joy and to be happy. Many are without dreams and goals. They like working a job but no big vision; they always think small.

Bill knew Mary's words were a lamp to his feet and a light to his path. A mate that he was always looking for (Psalm 119:105). One night at Bill's house, his brother called and told him his children had been looking for him. He had his phone on speaker and Mary heard it. Bill asked if he knew their phone number and address? He said yes and gave Bill all the information, to go see the children. Mary told Bill that he had told her that he didn't have kids and was never married before. So why did he lie to her? She explained to him that she doesn't have time for games and that she had been in two relationship that didn't work out. That in both relationships she put her all into them, stuck by both men, through thick and thin and yet they both hurt her feelings. She tried to love them, be their best friend and would have like to have married someday. She was glad she never married the first one because she might be on drugs and dead by now. The second relationship might have worked out because he did get his life back together. But she felt let down by a man that walked right out of her and her children's life.

But people come and go! That's the way love goes. Bill told Mary, he did have kids; he didn't claim them because the mother kept them away because he cheated on the kids' mom and ended up having more children by some other lady. Bill always loved his children and thought about them all the time. By not seeing them for years he just tried to block them out of his mind. Mary said, you told me that you would not lie to me! Bill claimed he didn't mean to lie but it hurt him not to see his children. He knew what he did was wrong but he did try to talk to the mother of his first children and told her he was sorry but she refused to give him another chance. The relationship ended and he had to move on and be responsible for the actions he took. Mary understood because no one is perfect, all are sinners and all have made mistakes. But we have to forgive and move on. Mary forgave him for that lie. Bill apologized to Mary and gave her a kiss.

Bill asked, Mary two years later if she would marry him? Mary said yes, I would love to. They got married, rented their homes out, got out of debt, bought a home together, and started saving and investing their money together. Bill and Mary had two children together. He was able to love the children unconditionally. His other children came over often and everyone got along. The house was big enough so if the kids wanted to stay sometimes, it was ok. A year later a gentleman came and asked did they want to own their own business? The two said, sure we would; if it's going to bring us wealth. Bill and Mary joined the business and can pay all their bills, save more and have plenty money invested. They are on the right path for retirement. Their money is growing and growing in the right mutual funds. Some of the children once they got old enough also joined the business. Mary taught other people how to have wealth and have their money working for them. Mary and her daughter also hold workshops for kids on how money works for kids. She wanted the kids to prepare early for retirement and retire early/at a young age. Retirement is not about the age; it is about how much money you can save and invest. Thing that the school doesn't teach children. The school teaches math, get a job after you finish school, go to college, but not how to build wealth and invest money. Bill and Mary had God in their lives and were wealthy, but they didn't let everyone know because it was not everyone's business. They just try to show people how to get what they desire and what was never taught in school -- and still isn't taught in school.

Mary and Bill never tried to impress people by showing off a car they have, a big house, going out eating, partying, traveling, or buying expensive clothing and shoes the way people sometimes do, even when they know they are in debt. They have seen people trying to keep up with the Jones. Buying things with credit cards and digging a bigger hole for yourself and the family, and getting into more and more debt, is always a bad idea. Just be who God made you to be because there is only one you and there are no two people that are the same. Avoid living beyond your means, stay in your lane and spend your money wisely. If you can't control your spending habits, not saving or investing, find yourself a professional coach. Just because you make a lot of money; avoid spending it all. You must know what to do with it and where to put it. The difference between the rich and poor is they know where to put their money. What do you think you and your spouse are going to have at retirement? There are so many people out in the world who make good money but have nothing saved for retirement. They feel they are doing great because they are able to pay all their bills and do plenty of other things. Please be mindful that you must save, invest, stay out of debt, get a budget sheet, don't be too proud to ask for help and get out of your pride mood.

Mary and Bill took the business offer that was given to them. Don't miss out on your blessing by being disrespectful and think you know everything just because you make good money. Instead, pile more information on top of what you know, from professionals who want to show you more. There are people who want to help and show you a better way to life. Get a professional coach, they know what they are saying and doing. Think about what you would want your family to have if something happened to you. Make sure you all have life insurance, most of the time it can save your home and get you out of debt. But you must know what is in your policy and how much. That is why you should have money saved too. You want to be able to pay off debts and keep your home, if your spouse is no longer with you.

Mary, after experiencing bad relationships growing up and how she just wanted to be loved, had endured a lot of pain. She did know, however, that her mom and God loved her. Women show love to the men most of the time and later get disappointed. Many have gone through this because we see other people happy and we want to be happy and cared for as well. We see the couple smiling, laughing, holding hands and it seems so sweet. But we can't see behind closed doors and many are crying in the dark and wish they never got into that relationship/

marriage. But you have to learn on your own; many stay stuck for a long time and for years. Their dreams are invisible. Women love so hard; and the men make their love come down, woo you make my love come down and making it come all the way down. The men know how to get a women heart. Women are so in love and can't live without that one love. One love, one love, you got to have that one love. That is how Mary felt too. But you have to love yourself first and let that man or woman know you aren't going to let them treat you any kind of way. Enough is enough. Did you see that movie (Enough), she got fed up with her husband messing around on her? Just because he worked and paid all the bills, her husband felt he could do whatever he felt like doing. Whether it was right or wrong. She tried to leave him, he refused to let her go and he wasn't treating her right. She did right, no one should have to put up with another human being who disrespects you and in front of your face or child. Children have a good memory and bad dreams. Watch out for your small children, who have seen you and your lover fighting or arguing. Especially if a man put his hands on you, hitting, beating or choking a woman. Watch your children's reactions; some children might follow you and cry for you all the time. The child can be spoiled or see things happen to their mom. You might not think of it that way but they can be crying on the inside; just like you. That is because they love their mother, fear for her life and feel the pain that she feels. Children can tell when something isn't right and it is harmful. They don't want anything to happen to you ladies. Be very careful of men who have put their hands on you more than one time and almost killed you. One time is enough because he might really take you out of this world. I know you love them and wish you could help them but if they don't have Christ and the right help that they need, you are putting yourself and the kids in danger. Children will be worried about you while they are away from you. It's so hard to say good bye to yesterday. Women, please be safe, think, get close to Christ and sometimes it's so hard to let go but you are not alone. Sometimes you have to say good-bye to the one you love. We are queens and deserve much, much better.

Sometimes we have to let go and let God do it! Just be careful, people are murdering the mother of their kids, the children and themselves.

Take what you see on the news serious, what a friend, family member, people who have been through what you have experienced, listen to positive leaders and take what they say, very serious. Mary had to think and take control of her reactions and be strong. It is so easy to keep holding on to something that causes us pain. So easy to do wrong and hard to do the right things. So easy to fall in love and hard to let go or get out. So easy to get married! But if you want a divorce, you have to go to the courthouse and pay. It can be hard to get out and it causes so much pain, when getting a divorce. It's easy to hold grudges and hard to forgive most of the time. It's easy to get pregnant and it can be painful when having a baby but can be hard raising children alone. It is easy for men to lie to women but hard to be faithful and tell the truth sometimes. People sign up for the gym and pay their money but it is hard to go work out; you waste your money and the gym gets rich for people not coming to the gym. (Proverbs 3:13) Happy is a man who finds wisdom, and a man who gains understanding. Be wise as a dove and have wisdom. (Psalm 55:6) So I said, Oh, that I had wings like a dove! I would fly away and be at rest. Many times, you may need to let go, fly away/walk away, in order to get rest and have peace. Please think before you keep accepting a man that abuses you in front of your kids or when you two are alone. Your children need you, your family loves you and so does Jesus Christ. Set goals for yourself and your children, if you don't have any. Refuse to let that bad relationship stop you from your vision.

Live life to the fullest and be happy. It is not over until God says it is over. Think about life and how you would want to live out the rest of your years. Life is short, so you don't have a lot of time to waste. Goals, dreams, vision and having a sense of direction is crucial these days. If you have gifts that God gave you, use them to help others as well as yourself. Maybe you have a gift to help people, be a leader, or service many human beings. We are all here for a reason, so help one another. It can be done in so many ways. We really are too blessed to be stressed, to beautiful to be beaten, to honest to be hopeless, to worthy to be wounded or worried and her body is a temple of God; not to be taken for granted. Keep pushing until you reach your goal, get out of the box with people who never move. Make your move right now, baby, you have to make that move. Walk your walk, talk wisdom and let nothing hinder you anymore! Not money, bills, relationships, marriage, children, family members and friends, etc. Bill and Mary are glad someone prayed for them. They are thankful for the Bible, basic instruction before leaving the earth, that is what the Bible means to them.

# Mary's Break Through

◇◇◇◇◇◇◇◇◇◇◇◇◇◇◇◇◇◇◇◇◇◇◇◇◇◇◇

Looking back over Mary's life, she had to make some major decisions. She had to think about was it good for her and was it healthy for the body and soul? Mary realized she needed God in everything she did and to ask Him to guide and lead her on the right path. She wanted to be free from roadblocks which seemed to drain her mind. Be set free from dead-end streets and refuse to keep walking like a blind bat. Get rid of people, places and things that are taking over your sight and covering your eyes. Find a new highway, path and direction that will lead you to glory. Mary had to get better daily, become wiser and be an example of what she wanted to do. That is when she began to unlock her full potential. She had to be careful who she went to for advice or opinion. God was her only and first choice because many people may not be qualified to give you the answer you need. She asked God to renew the right spirit in her and heal her soul from the past relationships. Avoid doing the same things over and over again; it would keep you in the same old habits and feeling unhappy. There are signs of destruction but many just can't see it or don't want to see clearly. God has been trying to get your attention, just like He was trying to get Mary's attention. Love can be so blind; you have to wake up some day and get the big picture. Wake up, everybody, no more sleeping away because time is passing you by and you are not getting better at all. Stop sitting on the dock of the bay, watching the time roll away. Count your blessings, get a vision and become your best while looking your worst. Keep on pushing, momma used to say take your time young children and don't rush to get old. Just live your life, live your life. Learn to make that move right now, baby, you got to make that move right now. We are too blessed to be stressed.

# Decision Needs to Be Made

◇◇◇◇◇◇◇◇◇◇◇◇◇◇◇◇◇◇◇◇◇◇◇◇◇

What kind of woman are you? Well dressed, kind, attractive, polite, show love, active in exercise, nice body figure, enjoy sports, like to cook, have things in order, a mother who keeps the house clean, take care of yourself and children, mature lady, honest, use encouraging words, treat others the way you want to be treated, or a woman of God who doesn't act on what the word teaches you. What kind of words come out of your mouth because your words defile a person? (Matthew 15:11). The words that come out of the mouth tell plenty about your attitude. Also read (1Corinthians 3:17), is your body a temple of God? Who are you serving? The world or God. What are you looking at? Who is your driver? Who is showing you the way, to get you headed in the right direction for a vision? We are our own product, when making our own decision. Make the right decision and pour your heart out to God. We are responsible for the decisions we make, what we speak and the things we do.

Don't look at what others have or try to be like someone else. Be yourself, we are all different in our own unique ways. We all have gifts that God has given us, all you have to do is put it to use. Your dreams are there for you; dream big dreams. Take the first step, everything else will follow and fall in place. When you say something, stick to it and let no one talk you out of it. You want to have a goal that can help the poor, homeless, give back to the community and be a role model. There are good men/women who are not good leaders. Who are you following? Children are watching you as well as others. Never give up because things take time. Say to yourself, I am never going to give you up, never going to give you up. At least you will be getting started moving out of the bad situation you were in, and begin wanting to do better for yourself. Always make yourself and your kids your reason to do better, in each season. There is nothing wrong with having a better life, better income, new thinking pattern, new friends, and mainly a better relationship with Jesus Christ. The problem is making your mind up, to be successful and have your own business. I got my mind made up, come on I can get it rolling anytime; today is fine and I am going to get my business rolling. Many of us doesn't want to work at a job for the rest of your life, knowing you hate the job, the boss and fellow employees. Know what is going on around you, especially if your goal, vision or dream can be a big help to all. Go for it and be that great woman/man sharing, being supportive and caring while giving ideas.

Be a lady who labors in her work at home or on a job. Lack nothing but get knowledge that would guide you to a vision. Climb the ladder to reach for bigger and better things in your life. Stop thinking small and letting the devil put you in a trick bag, instead learn to forgive all people because it will help you make some great plans. Be a lamp to other ladies, so they may see your light shine. Maybe then their darkness will come into the knowledge of true light. Remove lashing out at a loved one because of the past hurts. Never wait until it is too late to make peace with people you love. Leave the bad memories behind; the body needs to heal and be refreshed. Lift your head up, move from limiting yourself and go beyond your pain and make amends. Focus on that vision, move in authority, speak it, lose bad habits and show love. What are you longing for? What would you like to see happen in your life? Always walk in love, light, leadership, and in line with the word of God. Get wisdom and have freedom. If you want to be a very, very great leader be a true follower. Follow males and females who are making a difference in the world and in many people's lives. A leader who shows God's agape kind of love to many people. Being a great follower can help you become that awesome leader you desire to be. Keep moving toward your vision. If you need a mentor or coach, get one, they are an excellent helper to get you focused on that dream come true. They will tell you the truth and not sugarcoat anything and that is precisely what we need.

# WHAT'S STOPPING YOU?

◇◇◇◇◇◇◇◇◇◇◇◇◇◇◇◇◇◇◇◇◇◇◇◇◇◇

Avoid people who continue to hurt you, have your heart beating faster than a drummer. The men/women who don't want to be seen in public with you. Being a one-night stand or a bootie call in the middle of the night. Avoid men/women who always lie to you and use you! When they can't help or contribute to not one thing. You can get a wet tail anywhere but you are in love with people who don't care about you. They have already talked to their main chick and you are a side piece, who comes around in the darkness. What's that song, The Freaks Come Out at Night? Control yourself and stop letting any and every man put their thing in your tunnel. What's done in the dark, always comes out. Do you really think this is love? You were just a piece of leg hanging around until, they got the real person (man/woman) that they want. Some men already have someone, they just want their cake and eat it too. They used you because you let them. You knew they were with someone else but you refused to let go and hope he/she will one day come only to you. Many women know men who are married, but they still sleep with them. Get a life, get a vision, move on; stop crying over spilled milk and a piece of meat. Yes, it felt good for the moment, lasted only a few minutes but was it worth it? You are not alone. Some of you never meet the parents or family members. Even if you did, it still doesn't mean they won't cheat on you. Many let all their lady friends meet mom, dad and family because he thinks he's got it going on. They believe they are a mac daddy. No one should have to hide behind closed doors, living a secret life, hidden away like a ghost when you love a person with all your heart. Women, never allow any man to sleep with you, stay at your home, have a key to your home, eat your food up and you have children. Knowing he treats you like sugar, honey, ice, tea. Make sure he helps you with some bills. It is not fair for him to come in your house whenever he feels like it and you don't have a key to his home. You should be able to go to his house also and have a key. If he truly loves you and cares about you. Don't be no fool! If sex wasn't there to make you feel good; what would you do then? Are you a person addicted to sex, just have to have it? If so, you don't care who or how many men you spread your legs open to. Knowing that man won't provide for you and your children.

There are some women who will take care of these men first and forget all about their children. They leave their kids for a man. You just care about a good time, laughing and sex. Is this what you are showing/ teaching your child/children? Do you think it's alright, for a woman to take care of a man, even when he doesn't want to be seen in public with you, never wants to take picture with you and most of the time the men will come to the woman's house at night? Some women have left home, or left their children with a friend or relative to go stay or live with men. The problem is most of these men they leave their children for don't have his own place, mistreat you, have nothing to offer you and still live with their parents. Not all of them come at night; some men come anytime because they don't care who sees them. How does that make you feel; when a man treats you like that? You are supposed to be happy, surprised, it's like Christmas and Thanksgiving when he comes to see you? Do you call this love?

You are just a fool in love, remember it takes two to make everything all right. It feels good, yeah; it feels good! Won't it be nice to have him living with you and sleeping in only your bed? Having all of him! Would it be great for you and him to get married and you have him all to yourself? Together, forever; hopefully forever. The question is will you ever leave him? And most women say, no, no, no, and no. Learn to love Jesus like that because most of us love the material things of the world, and the things in the world. We need God to restore our soul. We are truly lost without Him and we settle for anything. Do you not see the Queen you are and your worth? Love can make people do some crazy, crazy things. We all just want to be loved but the best love comes from above which is our Lord and Savior Jesus Christ. He is nothing but love. He is all that and a bag of chips.

Get away from people who stress you out, make you angry and cause you to be bitter. Are you a person who curses all the time, gains weight, talk loud, loses weight because of stress, very disappointed with men, and angry because they left you for someone else? Guess what! You are not alone, plenty of women/men have been let down too! Stop holding hatred in your heart, hurting others because someone hurt you, and being confused. Get your mind right, focus on the number one person (God), wake up and run the race with the prize ahead of you. You are missing out on some amazing blessings that are in store for you. Stop wasting time on being miserable. Life is very short, enjoy life while you can but be careful how you enjoy it and with whom you do it. Pick your company wisely, a small circle of friends who want to see you have a much better life. People who are for you, not hurting you; we are missing a major part in our life and that is why we keep going back and forth to a miserable life or to that man/woman. God is missing, He is the answer to everything we need. God is trying to tell you something, God is trying to tell you something, right now, right now. When God calls you, please listen and never look back. When God calls, you better answer! He knows what is best for all of us. No, you might not know God and we don't know these boys/girls, male/female who get us frustrated and weaken our body either. We trust others and give them our heart, so why not trust our Savior; who is able to keep us from falling. A man that found a wife finds a good thing and women you also want to find a good honest man. (Read—Proverbs 18:22). So, try God, taste and see that He is good and there is no other on this earth who can do you the way He can, no not one. Make a change, the best is yet to come. Our Bible is Basic Instruction Before Leaving this Earth. It helps heal the body and mend broken hearts.

We meet strangers in a club, at the market, at a worksite, walking in the mall, playing in the park, at parties, over a relative's house, out with friends, online dating site, and at church, etc. It's funny how we fall so deep in love. We are not afraid to fall in love and are determined to have that love of our life. It is easy to fall in love and hard to get out of that relationship. Just like a marriage. Love at first sight and we don't even know them. Some relationships can mess up a person's eyesight for life. You can be in a relationship for years and still don't know a person. Know what you want out of life and see if who you are dating is on the same plane you are on and want to fly in the same direction. Let them know your plan and what you are trying to accomplish in the relationship. Refuse to spend more years with another person who doesn't want anything and has no goals. Women love hard and know what they want. It takes most ladies a long time to get over a man whom they trusted with their body. They know the relationship is a mess but hope things change. They try to hide their pain and hope no one sees the weakness inside of them. Women hide the broken pieces on the inside and are afraid to let go. You are a great male/female, try not to create something into your life that will damage your soul and mind. Adjust your lens and get the big picture for your vision. Always motivate, love, listen to your heart, forgive and take care of yourself first. Only God and you can take care of yourself better than anyone else.

The men/women cheat, lie, have babies by other ladies/men, many are disrespectful in front of others, stay out all night, they betray a person, sleep with other men/women at work which is a stab in the back. Why would you mess around with someone in the business with you, knowing you all are friends; then turn around and sleep with other ladies/men in the business? It is not just the men, the women too! They all want a taste of what the other women/men had or slept with in the business. Because they didn't want to see the other lady/man happy with that person or they didn't find what she/he was looking for yet, so she/he flirted with the male/female. Most of you are all friends, if a person already had a couple of women/men in the business, why would you want him/her? This happens in a lot of business and at jobsites. Some may want a person for the money or they just wanted to see how good he/she was in bed. Or to see if they could get that person, from another person? How did that make you feel, when you got that man/woman from your co-worker in the business or job? You think you were more woman/man than the other person? Never forget the same way you got that person is the same way you can lose them. There are other men/women in the world that are plotting also, just like you did. People can really get hurt by playing with other males/females' feeling. It can stop a male/female from moving ahead and from a vision. Please don't let anything stop you! We all have feelings. Learn to love yourself and stop trying to take someone else's partner. Just because you aren't close to people on your job, or don't hang out a lot together, you do talk to them, and it doesn't mean sleeping with the man/woman is OK, when someone else had them first. You all do business or work together. A respectful person wouldn't carry themselves like that. Get a vision and do unto others what you would want them to do to and for you. What goes around, will come back around. It can and will bite you in your tail. So, girls, you know you better watch out because some guys are only about that thing, that thing, that thing between your legs and some women just want some men for the same reason. Be careful who you treat wrong and smile in their face and stab in the back. Ask God to create a clean heart in you and just hope, He don't take your joy from you.

You don't want to be that lady who has to have a man. Which some act like boys and some women act like little girls. Jumping out of one relationship into another, from man to man, boy to boy and woman to woman; give yourself time to breathe. You cannot think well when your heart is troubled. If you have been in more than two or three relationships and they didn't work out, it means take time out for yourself and your children if you have any. It is not good to bring a lot of women or men around your kids, especially if you are not thinking about marriage. You can talk to people at a distance and not sleep with them, especially not everyone you meet, or they tell you that you are fine. Guard your body and your heart. Women, keep your legs closed and men keep your pants up. Get to know them, you will never know every detail. Some have demons inside, skeletons in their closet, hidden secrets and are Dr. Jackal and Mr. Hyde. Things you wouldn't want to know about because that attitude can change at any time. The side of a person that would put fear in the hearts of others and make you question them, saying to yourself, "this is not who I met." What a surprise, surprise, surprise this is what you fell for. Get up, pull yourself together and run, refuse to keep falling for the same love talk. Actions speak louder than words. Dream big, stop dreaming about a man, love yourself first and don't be a failure because that relationship didn't work. You allow fear to come in, fear of being alone and fear of thinking will I ever find Mr. or Ms. Right. It will come but be patient and take care of your body. Your body is the temple of God, not trash, it's valuable and worth something.

Know that you deserve better, stop feeling sorry for yourself and that man/woman who treats you bad. Get out of the pity party and get joy, peace and victory. Most people go to friends, family members and strangers trying to get answers. We ask questions like, what should we do, but don't take the advice. So, what is the use of asking, when you are going to stay stuck in pain. You have to get up enough nerves to speak out loud and say enough is enough, I'm sick and tired, I need to get off this merry go round, being a spinning top going around and around in a circle and getting the same results. Get up off that high horse and take control. You want a better life but are letting people stop you, it's called in love but love doesn't hurt. Loved ones are giving you the right encouraging words and it is up to you to make a move or stay broken down. Wake up, wake up, time is running out and doesn't wait for no one. Stop making excuses, procrastinating and let go of things that stand in the way of you getting a vision. Do some touching up, stepping out, grow up, learn to listen, and pray for a new beginning. Being nervous, clueless, blind, in a dark hole, in bondage (slavery in a relationship) and trapped is because of strongholds in your life. You are scared to move, used to being miserable and you think it is love. People, you are perishing because of a lacking knowledge. Refuse to listen to God, refuse to read the Bible, don't read positive books and avoid prayer. Most people have no clue; you are failing because of doubt, curses and uncertainty. Find ways to motivate yourself and become somebody. Listen to positive leaders, people who are going to tell you the truth, real women/men who are after God's own heart and want to be like God. That can change in your life.

Many are dating or seeing others and many have been in relationships for years and neither person has plans for their future. Some men are married or have a lady and you have been sleeping with that man for years; if they haven't married that woman or man, what makes you think they are going to marry you, nevertheless even leave who they are with, for you. Some of us are dating old flames, sleeping with all kinds of men, in and out of bed with them. And we know they are no good but are still sleeping with them and not getting a dime out of them. Here you need bills paid, need food, the kids need clothes and shoes, but you just want to feel good. There is going to be a time in your life when you make up in your mind to move forward and pick up the pieces to the puzzle that you've been searching for all your life. People will hate you, stop talking to you and will not share the truth; but there are people who are in the world, giving important information that everyone needs. People will talk badly about you because you are trying to do something awesome in your life. They are against the truth which professionals are trying to share. They don't understand the importance of what life is really all about.

Once they find their purpose and how to live right, it will be the best day of your life, so stop being clueless and get started on becoming successful. It's much better than being stressed, miserable, unwanted, unhealthy mind, bitter, and depressed all the time. No one should have to live in stress, it can kill you and bring sickness to the body. Start dreaming and follow people who are going somewhere and are headed in the right direction. If you stay in some of the bad relationships someone will eventually get hurt for playing with others' feelings. Jesus Christ has all the answers we need for our goals, dreams, vision and can help with bad situations. We don't have to stay in it and get the same result, where nothing is changing or getting better. Put your mind where the money is and get a vision. Jesus Christ wants to shape and mode us all. He is not going to force Himself on us because He wants us to come to Him in a time of need. Just ask, Him to come into your life and He will welcome us all in with arms open wide. He has so much love and peace to offer. Trust in Him and it will be all over in the morning because every day is a new day with Jesus Christ.

We cry that we are broke, have no money, living in darkness, fear has taken over and we are living paycheck to paycheck. The little money we have left, many still have nothing to save or don't know how to save. They have to spend every cent, then they need to borrow money from other people until their next pay. They have no life insurance, no savings, no 401k for retirement, no money for children's education, no future goals, renting all their life, never thought about buying a house and living off others/women. Never sat down and talked to their spouse about the future, what debt needs to be paid off, so they can get something they can own. Have people in your surroundings who know what they want, and can help you make the right choices that will lead to greatness. People have come to you, tried to show you how to make extra money but you wouldn't take time out to listen. Some of these products we need ourselves; but are rude. If men/women are showing you and it helps people, try it. Try new ideas and businesses because you should have more than one plan. More experience and knowledge under your belt, can help with your success. Listen, learn, grow and maybe one day you will lead others to a great opportunity. Never let anyone talk you out of something you know you always wanted to do.

Not your partner, kids, mother, father, family members or friends. You have to take care of you, never depend on someone else to do it for you, what you can do for yourself. If people are talking you out of something that helps others and everyone needs it, get away from them.

Shelly never talked her children out of a job or relationship, she let them learn on their own. Get a job if it brings money in, if it is clean money, doesn't harm anyone and it helps people. Mary's mother was very supportive. Because the money also benefited her too. A person shouldn't talk a child out of something that helps the world, especially if you are a grown man/woman, speak up for yourself. Take up your shield of faith and walk. Look to God to lead you. If it brings money into your home, money to help pay your bills, put food on your table and clothes on your back, go for it. Why wouldn't your family and parents support you, your child might have to take care of you one day, buy you a car or house. And if not, let them buy it all for themselves. Some people have listened to a parent, boyfriend/girlfriend, family, wife, husband and these people talk them out of doing something great in their life. Now the female/male are still struggling, and none of these people are paying their bills, not putting food on the table, haven't given them a dime and these are people close to them. But God is a friend to all of us, the one who can love you more, out of all the love or people in the world. He is a friend Who we can depend on and the one Who loves you more. Get His advice instead of a loved one's, if they are negative and against what you know will take care of you.

Everyone wants to live a better life. God has already given so many of us plenty of talent. What are we waiting for? Stop selling yourself short and get your business rolling. What do you have to lose? Get a small team, sit down and talk about what you all would like to do, and then get to the foundation of the business and make it work. Work for yourself, be your own boss, get up when you want, enjoy what you do and make this world a better place if you can. Reach out and touch somebody's hand, make this a better place if you can. Let people know they can become what they want, be good at it and succeed. Stop waiting, stop waiting, stop waiting and make that move right now, baby. Have faith and believe in your goal, vision and dreams. Are you thinking small? Yes, people are used to working for others and don't think they can make millions? Yes, you can. Set your mind on all the blessings God has in store for you. Sharpen the mind, get out of the problem because the mind is a terrible thing to waste. Listen, listen, wake up, wake up, mature and get the wealth which God has for us.

Relationships are one of the main reasons male/females don't have a purpose for their own business. Also, being around negative friends/family members who don't have dreams, don't want anything or never think big, can hinder your vision. You need that motivation and focus, not worry and pain. Get around dream makers who are making their dreams and goals come to life. Putting their words into action. We are responsible for our own actions that we take. How many people do you know who sit around with their family and talk about having a business? Not many, and you probably can count them on your right hand. Or maybe you can't count them, because you all never ever sat down and had a confession. Today, right now take a leap of faith, try new things and have your money working for you and your family. It is about that time, jump, jump, to it; you've got to make that move right now.

# Ways to Keep a Relationship or Marriage (Team Work)

◇◇◇◇◇◇◇◇◇◇◇◇◇◇◇◇◇◇◇◇◇◇◇◇

Put God 1st in your life, pray for a goal and vision
Being after God's own heart and dying to self
Do things God's way; not your own way
Listen to your heart and get a vision
Be kind and show love at all times
Love yourself, then you can love others
Have respect for yourself and other people
Dress nicely, not showing everything
Keep your hair done
Take care of your hygiene and keep your house clean
Be trustworthy, patient, tell the truth, and be honest

# Women's Stories

◇◇◇◇◇◇◇◇◇◇◇◇◇◇◇◇◇◇◇◇◇◇◇◇◇

STORY #1 Melody White

Melody White has four children, by one man which is her husband, Michael. They had been together for over 50 years. She's a woman of God, kind, polite, loves people and enjoys going to church. Her husband on the other hand was a heavy drinker. Michael never tried to stop Melody from serving the Lord. They had very little arguments because the Lord was working in and through Melody's life. They stayed together to death do them part. She was a wife, a mother, a cook and kept their house neat. Her and her husband worked all their lives and then retired. The marriage wasn't perfect but they took care of each other and loved all their children the same. She had some savings and retirement money; their vision was better than most people. What God put together let no one come in between the two. Marriage is a big step, it's not a game, not a fashion show or dress up day. It is when two people truly love one another from the bottom of their heart and to death do us part (it's forever). Staying together through rough times, hardships, arguments, disappointments, etc. God is key, to a peaceful life and a vision.

How Melody Was Able to Keep Her Marriage and Vision

Melody always put God first, in everything she did.
Went to church, no matter what the situation was at home.
Never changed her attitude or love for her husband.
Hung in there to death do them apart (to the end).
Still cooked and cleaned house.
Used wisdom and kindness at all times.
Her husband never stopped her for seeking God, never let friends, family or anyone hold you back from your goals or plan.
They communicated well together or as one.
No matter what, she continued to praise and worship the Lord.

## STORY #2—SHERA BROOKS

Shera was 65 years old and went to church. For some strange reason she ran into all kinds of men that were no good for her. They would abuse her with the words out of their mouths, telling her she was too old, walked to slow, nobody wanted her, etc., yet they were there in her life. Using her for her car, staying in her home, talked to her kids badly, and had all kinds of women in her car. Her friend Raymond would have her car while she stayed in the house, doing nothing and she even stopped going to church. This man put his hands on her and would always threaten to kill Shera. Especially when she tried to speak up for herself and fight him off of her. She called the cops a few times but would afterwards always take him back. Shera's life is so miserable, Raymond doesn't do anything with her, not even buy her anything for her birthday, Christmas, Valentine's Day, etc. She had friends but would only tell three of them how her man treated her. Her girlfriends stopped giving Shera advice because she would not leave Mr. Raymond alone. She was afraid of being alone, and was abused most of her life by men who she thought cared about her. Shera and Raymond both worked but he gave her no money and lived in her house. Shera claims she told him to get out plenty of times, but he wouldn't leave. Do you see how hard women love, compared to the way men love? Some men don't know how to care for or love a woman. Some women don't either. Get a vision and let go of things that hinder you. Stress will hinder you and will take you out of this world. Wake up, move on, get over it and tell Satan to get behind you. Bad relationships can stop you from your vision.

Shera Knew How to Make it Work

She needed Jesus Christ back in her life.

Speak up for herself, say what's on her mind and stick to her decision.

She needed to ask herself, is this how she wants to keep living; an unhappy life?

Where is her vision, goals and dreams?

Refuse to let men/women pull you away from Jesus.

People are only going to do to you, what you allow them to do.

Why keep letting all the pain and sorrow build up inside of you?

Avoid living in silence, hurting and let no one control you.

If you are not married, get out and run fast into the arms of your Savior.

STORY #3—Kelly Goode

Young attractive lady, nice long blonde hair, pretty eyes, and nice body shape. She's looking for Mr. Right, a handsome man, charming man, shows love and knows how to provide for a family. She had time to continue to be single, wait patiently, take care of her one child, and stay focused on her dream. The child's dad doesn't pay child support or help with any expenses. She experienced two bad relationships in her life. Kelly Goode has been doing well but help from the father of the child would make a big difference. She had to buy food, clothes, shoes, personal items, and pay rent. It's hard raising children alone and every parent needs to do their part (both men and women). This young lady worked two jobs, served God and likes helping others. Kelly had a vision, goals, dream; so that she can stop working at an early age. She wanted to be able to travel the world with her child. She is 23 now, how many young people think about getting their own business? Not many, they are stuck and can't find their way. Many young women are worried about boys/guys and having sex. Kelly wants to enjoy her life; she knows everything that she accomplished came from heaven above. She had a peace of mind, doesn't have to worry about being lied to, cheated on and stabbed in the back. Those two difficult relationships were a big experience in her life and she wishes it on no one. It leaves a person dry, weak, lonely and unable to focus on anything. Not a dream, a job, and it keep you away from your goal. Kelly shares her goal with old and young people, on how to own a business but very few people listen.

Kelly Made Her Goal Work

She had to get her thinking and mind straight, #1 focus on the higher power (God).

Her business and her child were, her why.

Kelly learned her lesson and kept her eyes on the prize and always prayed.

Learned to be very patient and never gave up.

She didn't bring men around her child, her trust was in Christ.

Worked hard now and in your older days; you can work less or have money working for you.

Kelly's child was more important than a man, avoid letting a woman/man weaken your soul.

STORY--- #4 Cynthia Code

There are many women who dated someone at work. Cynthia remembers her ex-boyfriend telling her to never date or fool around with a person on her job. Did Cynthia listen? No, she didn't. She started dating Heavy at the worksite. He had two kids and Cynthia had no children. They were seeing each other for five years. The man was still sleeping with the children's mother. He also was messing with other women on the job but Cynthia was so blind she couldn't see it. She really liked this man and he was using her, until he got what he wanted. God gives us plenty of signs but we as women/men are sleepwalking and don't want to see the light. Something is wrong with that picture. When you only go over his/her house at night, you are just a bootie call or night chick. He never gave her money, refused to take her out in public or be seen in the light with her. Heavy started acting like he was doing a lot of overtime at work. But instead, he was trying to let the other three ladies down easy, on the job, which Cynthia had no clue. He called Cynthia a few times, saying I love you and miss you. Which was a lie because he stopped coming around her, and never spent no time with Cynthia. Who wants a person like that? That's right, that should have hit home or opened a person's eyes but we are madly in love, right? Still in the pit and living in the darkness. Cynthia let go, she didn't let it stop her from her vision. Heavy really played a game on Cynthia and it hurt her to know how sneaky and disrespectful he was to her. He never said, sorry! Cynthia is waiting patiently on God. Relationships can and will confuse a person's heart.

How Cynthia Handled the Disappointment

She kept her cool at work, so no one would know what happened.

Cynthia saw how Heavy was like a snake and real sneaky.

Cynthia said she could never do that to a person with whom she worked. Even if they weren't the best of friends.

She also realized it wasn't worth fighting for; she continued moving toward her vision.

God has something much better in store for her life. Her trust is in the Lord.

Staying single-minded and focused, hitting her goal and no stress, feels great.

She thanks the Lord Jesus Christ for what she's been through because if she didn't go through anything, she wouldn't have known what the power of God could do.

Women/men, if something is holding you back from success, causing stress, let it go. You are not alone.

Choose your circle of people with discernment, wisely and use the wisdom God gave you.

## STORY #5---Tina Keys

Bill and Tina met at a funeral home, where Bill worked. Tina was on the shaky side and was losing her mind. Each one of her children's dad left her for other women. Didn't let her know anything, they just left out the door and never came back. She found Bill, the older man, and he wanted a younger lady and Tina wanted him. Things was going well for two months until she found out he was married. The wife was in her way and she wanted her removed from Bill's life fast. About three months later, Tina paid someone to kill the wife and the police never knew what happened to Bill's wife. Tina didn't have him long either, he was dead one year later. He knew what Tina did to his wife and he did suffer for the hidden secrets. Tina is also suffering for taking that woman's life. Tina passed away about six years later. We can't hide from God. Avoid thinking negative things because crazy love can cause your attitude to turn into corruption.

### Tina Had No Vision

Tina should have found her own single man and not someone else's husband.

She had no goal or vision, she was perishing away with bitterness.

Avoid getting so mad that you have to take a person's life. Jail is no joke or place to go.

Negative decisions can drive you crazy and away from a goal or vision

She needed God and still hadn't seek His face never and still didn't seek God before she died.

A man/woman with no dreams, in pain, miserable, they don't care if a person is married.

God sees everything and we all have to stand before Him.

Tina didn't like being the other lady and should have walked away. It is not worth taking a life. There was no money in it for her.

Story #6---Sue Hampton

Sue on the other hand did meet nice guys. They would take her out to eat, go party, went to see movies and travel often. The problem was none of these men were interested in her four children. The children were young ages 3, 4, 7, 9 and were well mannered and respectful. Ms. Hampton still went out with the men until one day, she met a gentleman who asked for her number. He was dressed nicely, polite and had no kids. She explained to him she had four children and they were her life. His name was Emanuel, he said he had been watching her for over two years and that she looked beautiful. He stated how he was looking for a wife, someone he can trust and he can take care of. Sue told him to let her think about going out with him because she had a couple of friends. He told her to take her time and please get back in touch with him. Sue was no dummy, she got rid of the other guys and took him up on that offer. Now they have been happily married for over six years and he just loves Sue and the kids. They are just getting ready to have their first child together. What a blessing! You have to know when the right person comes into your life. A lot of times women/men miss out on something great. They have their goals, which they are working on together as one, for the future.

Sue had a dream

She knew marriage was the commitment she always wanted.

A gentleman who would love her and her kids; they both are on the same path of wanting their own business together.

Sue found a person that thinks like her. Both had a goal and plans for their future. Both had plans to retire early.

They made sure that if anything happened to either one of them, the children would be taken care of, as well as the other spouse.

Most young people don't think about leaving their child with an inheritance, if they passed away. It's hard out here: get things in order, life is too short.

The couple feel they are truly blessed by God.

Stop settling for less, ladies/men, you deserve better and should be treated like a queen/king.

Both parties were on the road to peace and joy. Won't God do it? He can work it out for you too.

STORY #7---Gloria Frank

Clueless, clueless when you can't seem to catch on to being used. Gloria has a nice male friend who gives her money, without her asking him; but she like the guys that ask her for money. She always gave the men her dollars and they only sleep with her sometimes. Next thing you know, she never sees them again. She sleeps with anybody and even boys younger than her. They only come near Gloria when they need something from her. Gloria has lost two men, who like her personality and the way she dressed. She didn't want them, she was interested in the wrong men, all her life. She was used to being used and doesn't know a good thing, even if it smacked her in the face. Gloria messed around with so many men and they didn't want her at all. Those are the guys that she liked. John was a good friend (man) who gave her money, she thought he just wanted to sleep with her but he was the one who truly liked her. She knew that was all the other men ever did and wanted her money. She didn't want John, and the relationship ended. She was blind and clueless. She is still picking up bad male friends. She wants to marry someday but she needs to choose wisely.

Gloria Needs True Love

Ms. Frank was clueless and didn't realize when the right man comes her way.

John really cared for Ms. Frank but she's blind when it comes to love.

Know what you have when it comes your way. She missed out on a good thing.

Know your worth and who you belong to.

Having low self-esteem, has you going around in a circle.

Ms. Frank needs to wake up and know what kind of man she needs in her life.

STORY #8—Kimberly Banks

Being married three times, Kimberly still noticed that even men at her age or older are still playing games and telling lies. Kimberly is 59 years old, and just started dating one of her old flames again. She left him alone for lying and playing games fifteen years ago and just got back with him again. He is still living with a woman and fooling around. Gary is trying to sleep with Kimberly again. Why do women like to be the other lady or second in line? They both have nothing, no home of their own, he can't provide or take care of Ms. Banks or give her money. He can't stay out late or take a vacation for the weekend or a week with her. But he told Ms. Kimberly that he and the lady live together, sleep in different beds and don't get along. Gary lies, he will never change and will never leave that lady. Ms. Banks needs to stop settling for less and know that she can do better. Gary got caught talking to Kimberly on the phone and that was the last time Kimberly heard from him.

Let Go of Old Bad Apples

Avoid going backwards, or to the same broke person.

Do you want to live better or worse?

Build your foundation while you are young. Have a saving account, 401k, 457, investments and life insurance.

Avoid being broke and without a home that you can call your own. You are going to need plenty of money at retirement.

Get out of the habits of being the side piece of meat. Some of us are too old and have nothing to offer. In your older life; you should be enjoying life and not complaining broke.

## STORY #9--- Michelle Tyler

When dating a married man or a man who is sleeping with other women besides you, be very careful. Because most of the time you will stay the side piece. Most married men stay with their wives, even when they get caught fooling around. Michelle is a witness of both. She was determined to get this man who worked at the Post Office. One day Ms. Tyler approached the man and later they started seeing each other. The people on his job knew he was married but noticed Michelle was coming around him a lot. This went on for one year and two months. One Friday, Michelle and Thomas went to Pizza Hut and his wife's best friend was there but she was in the bathroom. The two got a seat and sat at the table, in Pizza Hut. The best friend saw them together and called the wife. The wife came, she sat in her car until they came out and started swing her knife. She cut the husband across the chest, in the back and on the arm. The married man is still alive, still lives at home, never pressed charges and is still seeing the other lady. Michelle should have left the man alone because this could have been worse. Michelle refuses to leave Thomas alone.

### A Wake-Up Call for Michelle

God is trying to get both Michelle and Thomas' attention.

Many people's vision is very blurry and darkened.

Their focus is on the wrong thing. Michelle wants what she wants, even if it causes a divorce.

They both had an opportunity to sneak around and found pleasure by sinning.

It is how you live your life and how you carry yourself. If you don't care and are giving your body for free, a man is going to go for it.

Michelle is living a dangerous life because of her obsession with her lover.

She has a desire for a man who belongs to another woman.

Get a man she can call her own. Remove everything that may cause disappointments.

Story #10---Paula Smith

Paula had a few good friends from school in her circle, who wanted to help her. Paula is one who never worked and thinks others are to give her money and do for her that which only she can do for herself. Her girlfriends have tried to help her get a job and show her how to have her own business. Paula would learn the business, start studying and stop. She complained, saying her boyfriend made her mad, just when she was ready to start the business. She wants to make money and have her own but make so many excuses. Never use people as a crutch. It can cripple your thoughts and keep you from thinking for yourself. Her relationship that she is in, stops her from moving ahead in life. She's very unhappy with the lies and cheating but she is madly in love. She always wanted advice from her wealthy girlfriends but she never listens. We all know what we should and shouldn't do. They stop giving their opinion because it goes in one ear and out the other.

Getting Help for Paula

Paula is struck in a love triangle.

She needs to get out of the relationship and learn to love herself first.

Find someone who will treat her as a queen, a lady and not a child.

Find someone who can love her the same way she loves him.

Paula needs to open her eyes and get to the root of her problem. She's in her own way.

She needs to stop letting fear stop her from making money and taking care of her children.

She will never have momentum. If she doesn't move, she will continue to be time broke and money broke.

A true friend will tell you the truth. Most of us are scared of the truth.

Paula needs to let God be the leading person in her life and to guide her.

# LIFESTYLES---- PEOPLE ARE USED TO

◇◇◇◇◇◇◇◇◇◇◇◇◇◇◇◇◇◇◇◇◇◇◇

Many people all over the world are blind, and can be ignorant because of lack of knowledge, rude, disrespectful, unloving, not caring about your family and think small. Most people are afraid to think big, think they can never have their own business because we are so used to working for companies. It would be nice to work and do what you want to do and get up when you feel like it. What do you think you can do to provide for people's needs and help your country? Start searching and coming up with ways to make money for you and the family. Had your boss ever given you a book to study and show you how to own a business like him, so you can someday have a position like him? If not, you will be working for the rest of your life on the clock. But that is the only thing we were ever taught to do: work for others and never reach the top. It is sad but it is time to wake up and get a vision. In school many of us never learn about savings, retirement, life insurance, and how money can work for us and not against us. We can have our money taking care of the family if something happens to the adult/parent. There are people out here who are passing the information on but we refuse to listen. Listen so you can mature, grow up and have wealth! Become motivated when others share free knowledge, take it all in and follow the direction they give you. You might figure, "Oh, I can't do this," but you can indeed make your money work for you. Come from behind the doors of the past history, how we lived back in the 1920s and become a business owner.

Why stay pointless, no sense of knowledge, no vision, no hope to do anything, no dreams, no desire, no future plans, no savings nor life insurance and no purpose for your life. It is being useless. It is serious when you work and get paid less for a job that should pay more money, and the bad part about it is you hate the job. Can you see where your money went or what you spent it on? Do you have a budget plan and are you writing down what bills you pay on each week? You have to change things around and create something worth working for. Few men/women can't keep a job, some are just lazy and many don't work because their parents never made them go get a job. Some men don't work because they owe child support and Social Services might take most of their check, because they owe money to the children's mothers. But you need to step up and take care of the children.

It took two bodies to create and bring a child into the world, so they are yours too. Men, are you living with other women, and are you helping them? What about money for the kids' mothers; after all, you helped make those babies. They need help as well. Are you sleeping around making more kids and haven't helped with the ones you already have? Be a man and do your part, these kids didn't ask to be here. Men/women with children should want to spend more time with their children and family. Try listening to others who once worked just like everyone else but are millionaires now. They are spreading the word around but no one wants to hear, and this is the same about Jesus Christ. No one wants to hear the Lord's name until things get out of control, when things hit home, when something happens badly to a loved one or when we are on our deathbed. That is when we want to call on His name and go to Jesus in prayer. We have to call on Him daily, also pray all day for peace for the world, for ourselves, for families and pray for everyone.

Ladies/gentlemen have been talked out of their vision by their spouses, friends, mom, dad, boyfriend, etc. Women, speak up, why are you letting human beings tell you not to do things you know you want to do or God put it on your heart? You are up in age where you can make major decisions for yourself. When you were a child you spoke as a child and now you have grown up. (1 Corinthians 13:11) Be that man, wear those pants in your home and speak up. Most of you are working and paying the bills, so why not try something that can make your own hours and your life much easier. Let them know, I am tired of working for people and it's time to step your game plan up. Go with your heart and get away from people that don't want to be happy for you or help you with the decisions you make. Become a role model, leader, a people person, offer your help and do it with a kind soul. There are plenty of things the world can use, so what vision do you have in mind? What can change the life of a person? One thing, always tell people about Jesus Christ. How can you and the world be happy with your product? As you can see from all the reading so far, that relationships of all kinds, are the one reason that keep us in bondage. The relationship has caused us depression, hurt, pain, weakness, bitterness, brokenness, anger, and made us mad and messed up our mind. When you let things destroy the mind, the pain gets stronger and remains hidden in the body until it is exposed. When the last button gets push, everything in you comes out like a bomb. Blowing everything up and whatever is in the way. There are many things you have to get away from, in order to see the vision inside of you. You have to be tough and use tough love on people; you can still love them, even when telling them bye-bye, move out of my way.

Another thing that holds us back or stops us from a vision, are blind spots in our own lives. We are so busy looking at who hurt us, who left us, why, when, if I would have, what I could have done, and should have done in the relationship or marriage. All these things take our mind off of, who is really the problem here? Most of us are our own problem, we make problems for ourself instead of letting the past go. Change your mindset, the attitude, people, places, things and direction. Now is the time to do great things and start climbing to the top. The sky is the limit, so how high can you go with a dream, vision or goal? Many of us have a beautiful heart on the inside but are not good role models for people. Look in the mirror, what do you see? Check yourself out before blaming others for your mistakes. Take responsibility for what you allow in your life. Every person needs/should have their blind spots removed and healed. You must deal with them head on. You are a wounded person with unbelief. What you focus on is what you become and what you listen to is what will come out of the mouth. As a man thinks in his heart, so shall he become (Proverbs 23:7). Make up in the mind to have a better life, start today because it is never too late. Blind spots are so dark inside of the body and a person doesn't realize it. It hinders the mind and stops the body from moving forward. Ask the Lord for His help. The past has kept us locked down in a cell for so long, that it has us thinking about the past hurt and feelings. It blocks the blessings the Lord has for us because we are so blind that we know nothing about blind spots. Blind spots keep the mind black and there is a deep hole in our heart. Break those chains and be set free. You will be able to think much better and be open to free knowledge and more. Get a Vision.

Maybe you are empty inside and have no clue which way to run. When the body is empty, the devil knows he can take advantage of your life. It is because you are weak, dry, lonely, confused, need love, unhappy, bitter, and your thinking is off in the wind. You don't know if you are coming or going. You want out and you want to stay in the bad relationship or marriage. Cleanse the body out, get all that junk and mess out of your system. (Psalm 51:2). We do things, listen to the wrong people and we knew better but we did it anyway. Leave it behind and never look back. Be transformed from darkness into the light. It's time to wake up and run the race to victory. We all have some good in us and we have a talent, so use it now. What are you sitting around waiting for? You are a gift. Refuse to be a double minded person. One minute you want to work for yourself and the next minute you think it is impossible to have greatness or a business of your own. Double minded people get excited about a plan, then someone comes along and talks them out of it. (James 1:8, 4:8). You have nothing to lose but so much to gain and share. Avoid listening to people who don't have anything. Always take a chance at things that will benefit you and the family. Listen to professional men/women who know what they are talking about. Always get a comparison or more than one opinion. Most of the time we listen to the wrong people and when the right business man/

woman comes along telling the truth, you won't change what you have been or are doing because we've been taught the wrong information for a lifetime. It is time to wise up and get the right knowledge, discernment and wisdom. You have to know, when the mind tells you this is for you, without others telling you what to do. Always do what is best for you and what you know is right in God's eyesight.

Another thing that holds many girls and boys back are strongholds. Holding on to that dear old hatred, pain and attitude. Blaming others for your behavior. Only the person himself and with God's help, can control their own habits (good, bad). When looking at the past feelings and hurt, get rid of them because until you forgive and let go, the stronghold will never leave you. What you think about all the time, is what controls you. If you are mad with someone, stress, worry and talking bad about that person, it is taking up all your time. There is no time for a vision, for God, a plan, a goal or dream because you are wishing bad luck on others. While talking about others, what are you doing with your life and what do you have for retirement? A mind focused on Christ, has no time for stress and bitterness. Many are still stuck in neutral; when are you going to change gears? Stop having a pity party with yourself and the men/women are out with someone else. They are not even thinking about you but you are upset with the world over something small. Get out or over the feeling. Stop living in your feelings. Forgive family, friends, loved ones and neighbors. If not, you are tied down to a stronghold. Being miserable week after week, month after month, and year after year; still in the pit. Loosen everything that is making you frustrated and unforgiving. Focus on you and make that move right now. What's love got to do with it? Remember that song! Your vision is calling you to wake up. (John 14:1) Let not your heart be troubled. How long will it take you: 50 years for something you can do in a day, walk away and forgive? What is taking you so long to shift? The Bible tell us our life on earth is until 70 years old and if you live longer; what a blessing (Psalm 90:10). Time is running out and you are trying to fit in with angry people to harm others. You must redeem your time, stop misusing time on the past and focus on wisdom (1 Cor. 7:29-31).

Most young/old people abuse time, misuse time, backslide, their eyes affect their life and they are wasting opportunity.

Some ladies/men don't have a vision because they refuse to change. Many procrastinate while dealing with old disappointments that happened years ago and others just enjoy getting treated bad. Thinking that is love, first we break up, then we make up that "game for fools." Remember that song! How about the song, "It Feels Good"? Many believe that is real love! It's just an unhealthy relationship or marriage. Wouldn't it feel great to see and live life to the utmost, making dreams come true? Be thankful and happy, expressing love with that one special lover who cares for you, like you love them. He/she is waiting patiently once you let go of that sour lemon. Why are you staying with someone who makes you feel unwanted and has you worrying? Try being happy without a person like that, put off the old man and make a change (Ephesians 4:22-24). Walk in love and get your freedom back. Take back everything the devil stole from you. Then the dreams, goals, plans, and vision will come creeping in and help you see again. The vision is cloudy, start wiping your eyes, from crying so much over spilled milk and they don't even give a darn about you. Why are you procrastinating, when others are trying to help you move up in the world? You don't want that positive answer; you want what you want whether it is good/bad for you. You are in love, so in love, it stopped you from working and having a plan. You feel if loving you is wrong, I don't won't do right! I don't want to do right! Remember that song? Wake up and put on the whole armor of God. Be a decision-maker, by making good decision that helps you get on the road to purpose. Then you can sing, Victory is mine, Victory today is mine, I told Satan to get behind me and Victory today, I'm living my life.

We mess up when we put people before God. (Mark 10:27) tell us, with men it is impossible but not with God, for with God all things are possible. When it seems hard to let go of someone, it's like you are in jail or held hostage. Is torment a good feeling of love? Looking through wallets, phones and knowing he/she is sleeping around. How does that make you feel? A person shouldn't have to do this; if they trust each other, but we look because they give us reason to know/think they are up to no good. No trust and no communication, meaning, no relationship at all. Many are just their building up more strife, envy, and stirring up lots of hatred. Which leads to a dangerous mind and thinking negative thoughts. The Bible says, give no place to the devil, but a lot of us do and Satan gets the best of our inner soul. (James 4:7, Ephesians 4:27). He beats us down so bad that we can't get back up. When serving God, we may fall down but we can get back up again, get back up again, we fall down but we get up. Women/Men, are you sitting around having confession about relationships with friends and family? Did anything get resolved or did you all get to the real problem, the root of the problem? Was the problem you, and you like the way you feel because you are in love? Don't just talk about these things and never accomplish anything. Everything isn't funny, it is a time to mature, grow up and stop letting people take advantage of your body and mind. Broke people do these things because they have nothing better to do. They call this fun time but stay in pain because of a dead relationship. Never talk about a business, how to get more money, more income for the families, teach their kids the value of money, never talk about retirement and who is on the right track for the future. Broke people just don't talk about success or have a plan. All they talk about is how broke they are and how they have no money.

They don't talk about a solution to their problem because they feel it is impossible to have a good amount of money. In relationships, they don't want to be alone, empty inside, can't find their way in life, use government benefits which make a person lazy and depend only on the government for help. You will never grow or have more money that way, so if you want better you have to decide in your mind. I can have much more if I put my mind to a vision and ask God to help lead me. Many of you are with men/women who want to just sleep with you, see you when they want, lie all the time, never take you to their place, never want to be seen in public with you, lay their seat back when they get in your car, so no one can see them, have a key to your home and you will never get one to their place. How does that make you look and feel? Avoid letting a person make you feel that you are not worthy, not a Queen or a King because you are. You must let a lot of things in your life go because you are missing out on some amazing things God want you to explore and have. He has a better way for everyone who is going through pain/suffering. He has a whole new ballgame and wants you to be on His team. He is the new coach/sheriff in town. Men/Women, we as adults must teach our children because they might do what they see you doing. Be a good example for your daughters and sons. Do you want to play on God's team? "God is so good!" It took most people years to understand, that we have the power to get out of dead, beat-up relationships. God was missing and we refuse to listen to Him! We listen to our own heart. Do some touching up, be determined, focus on you and get a new lifestyle. Stop behaving the way you do because you are just making yourself sick. Be very serious about a goal, impacting the lives of people and the world. Get out of this "slavery of love," that "if loving you is wrong, I don't want to do right!" Having God's love, can lead you to self-love and everything will start making sense. Get to the bottom of the corruption in your life, before it explodes. You are not alone, other have experienced worse.

# Teach Your Children While they are Young

◇◇◇◇◇◇◇◇◇◇◇◇◇◇◇◇◇◇◇◇◇◇◇◇

Teach your children while they are young, to save money, budget money, and own something that they can call their own. We haven't been taught much about money in school but we were told to go get a job. Parents, if you have a coach who taught you about money, let your children know and that way they can teach their kids. Many people never thought about a coach and feel they don't need one but if you want your child to make their first million, get a good coach. Listen, there are a lot of things you don't know or didn't understand and you will need that knowledge. It is a need, if you want to be set for a lifetime. You should want the kids to learn about wealth early and keep it going from the next generation to the other generation that follows. Teach them about Jesus Christ as well! He plays a big part in helping you meet that goal. You need to know children, how to have money, working on your behalf and in your favor. Build your income, put it in the right stocks and bonds, protection for their family and have life insurance, these things are so important in life today. Avoid letting your life insurance policy to lapse, especially during the Coronavirus outbreak. Not just that, always keep it active. The world has changed for the worse and we will need to be prepared, secure, and protected. People are leaving this world fast. The faster they come in, the faster they disappear and have no coverage to take care of the family (wife, kids or husband). Please be mindful and get your life and house in order. This is serious business: don't leave your family without anything or have them struggling. Many have worked all of their life; some have nothing to show for their hard work and still struggle. They have no car, house and no savings. Our young children need to know, so they could have something of value and know it belongs to them. We have to break the curses, from years of history. We can have our own business but you must think positive. Read books, listen to mature adults and people who want to see you have a goal or dream come true. It is never too late; God has something in store but He must hold it until you recognize the things that have been weighing you down. Your blessing is waiting for you! (Proverbs 22:6). Train your boys/girls in the way you should have them go and they will remember what you told them. You don't want them to make the mistakes we made but learn, grow, mature and build wealth.

As parents we were taught to send our kids to college after high school. Get a degree, a Master's degree and other degrees. Boy/Girls have got degrees but still have a hard time finding jobs. Did you know college deals with our mind, the way you think and the way the brain works? We all will need the Bible, it deals with our heart. There are some professional companies in the world, where you don't need a degree. All you need is to read up on some knowledge, take pre-tests, next the final test and you can get your license to become a millionaire. But most people quit to fast because they don't want to put the work into it. No matter what you do you will have to work and put a lot of time into your dreams. We are used to working a job, until we retire. Most of the older people are still working, they can hardly walk and have no money saved. You don't want this to be you or your children. When you get older, you should be traveling and enjoying life. There are a few jobs, where you can work on your own time and work from home. Always appreciate what you are doing in your life. But if it isn't really what you want to do, find ways to get what your heart desires. Always listen, try new ideas, meet new people, and get the heavenly knowledge. Be wise. Proverbs 22:17 says; Incline your ear and hear the words of the wise. And apply your heart to my knowledge. For it is pleasant when you apply it to your soul and mind. When business people come to you, have an open ear to hear and think about what you heard. If you don't want to do it, share the information if it was good. We should all want to always open a business that would benefit the world.

Make sure the children follow Jesus. He is the way, the truth and the life while we are still living on this earth. It will help make their lives much easier and help deal with different hardships in life. Never talk bad about the other parent. Instead, get them to make peace with each other. Tell them about the Bible—base information before leaving the earth. (Proverbs 22:6) Train up a child in the way he should go. The Bible is our living guide, direction, light and gives us a vision. God is love and it can help our children learn to love them self and love others. Teach a child about church, let them know don't look at the people in church but go to hear the word of the Lord. Everyone that goes to church, are not there for God's word, and many stop other persons from going to church because of their ways and attitudes. Read the Bible for yourself, because some Pastors are not right but there are a few good Pastors. Many think Bible College is the #1 because it deals with our heart and God's agape kind of love. How many of us need Bible College for our heart and need it in all of the schools? People are killing in schools, markets, churches, homes, harming others and kill themselves. These are places we are supposed to be safe but people have (dangerous minds) unhealthy minds. Have your mind renewed and never repay no one for evil (Romans 12:10,17), you want to do good things to everyone. The Bible is food to the soul, and healthy for the body and mind. It can change your life and it is everlasting life. Children and adults, it is time to get a vision, making dreams and goals come to life. We need the love of God in our hearts because people are suffering and dying. What are you waiting for or waiting on? WAKE UP! WAKE UP!

WISDOM
ANALYTICAL
CANDID
FAIR
HONEST
CLEAR
PERCEPTIVE
DECISIVE
WISE
POWER
strong
courageous
confident
tenacious
absorbed
patient
valiant
bold
VISION
grateful
inspired
beautiful
creative
joyful
humble
observant
FEELING

# Story About Men/Boys

◇◇◇◇◇◇◇◇◇◇◇◇◇◇◇◇◇◇◇◇◇◇◇◇◇◇

Story--- #1 Tim Brown

Tim has been alone for years and has no family. He had been finding women who didn't love him and were only after his money. He was so kind, had bumps all over his body and had pretty hair. He had his own car, house, and was retired. For years he was alone and wanted someone to love him, for what was inside of his heart. He wished people would avoid looking at his skin and respect his heart. When he went to kiss the last girlfriend, she was scared of him and almost threw up. He told her, "My bumps won't hurt you! Why can't you love me?" She said, "I can't do it," and she walked out the door. He was so hurt and still looking for love. Shelly came along because a friend told her, Tim Brown had plenty of money. They started dating, but when Shelly saw him, she wasn't sure if she could put up with the bumps. But she knew he was a gentleman, by the way he talked. She tried to overlook the bumps and they stayed in the relationship. She was kind of homeless and really needed the help. Shelly did what she had to do and they got married four years later. Tim was very happy and believe it or not, Shelly grew to love him for the rest of their life. That's love!

Tim found love

Tim found a woman who overlooked his bumps

He found a lady who treated him the same way he respected her.

Do the right thing by one another!

His vision for a lady came to pass.

You want a person to love you for who you are, not thinking they are going to get something out of you.

The couple is happy and show love to one another

Story #2---Brian Glover

Brian wanted nice things, a big home and a man cave. But he had no plan on how to get it. Brian lived most of his life off of women. Women who had their own apartment or house and didn't care where they lived as long as he could lay his head down. He didn't want to be alone. He loved to work but never had anything to show for his hard work. He only showed and talk about how tried he was every day. Who wants to live their life like that! The money he brought home did pay some bills, and there was none to save at all. He lied to women a lot and was a cheater. He needed to get his priorities, responsibilities and life in order.

Brian Never Had His Own

Brian needed to know his Why. Why he didn't have money after all these years or his own place.

Find a nice lady and settle down.

Learn to tell the truth and stop playing games with ladies' feelings.

What goes around, comes back around.

His parents were good role models. However, you can have good parents as role models, but some children just don't follow in their footsteps.

He needs his priorities lined up, and then think about having a lady of his desire.

Listen to professional people who can help him budget and save his money, so he is able to care for himself and a wife someday. Be able to own something and call it his own.

Story #3---Wayne Strokes

Wayne Strokes had a vision for playing music, wanted to sell houses, sell fish, and wanted to be a Pastor. Most of these he didn't accomplish because he refused to stick to them and gave up too quickly. He is a man that has his own and provides for the family. He's always tried. He always been halfway on the right path. The only thing is he stopped seeing his older children, from his first relationship; before he got married, he would always see the kids. He stayed single for years and his full attention was on God. After the marriages, his first kids' hearts got broken, by a man they called Dad. Never let anyone stop you from doing what you know is right, in the eyes of God. It hurt Wayne as well because he didn't know his wife was going to switch up on him and didn't want to accept his first children.

Wayne Needs to Express his Feelings

Always keep God first and take control of your household.

Never disconnect with any of your children. If you already had connection and things were going well, please continue the relationship!

Learn to talk to your spouse. If there's no communication, you have no relationship.

Avoid abandoning your kids because it takes time, weeks, month, and sometime years for them to trust you with their heart again.

Learn to speak up as man of the household.

What are you fearing or waiting on, to make amends with your children?

Are you hurting on the inside and know what to do but refuse to do what is right?

## Story #4-- Harry White

There was a male named Harry, and he had two children by Betty. This man would get so drunk, call Betty out of her name and throw things in the house. She was a nice house mother of two and loved herself some Harry. She would go in a corner and just cry. Harry was fine, loving and caring as long as he wasn't drinking. He truly did love Betty and the children. He wasn't lazy and went to work. They both worked but had no vision or goals. Harry didn't spend much time with Betty and the children. They were living paycheck to paycheck and struggling with their finances. They do travel sometimes with family and love all their family members. The couple got married and have been together for over 22 years now. Harry just doesn't have his priorities in order, professional men/women have come to them but they turn down the help.

## Harry and Betty Need Help

If they had a professional coach, and a business, they could spend more time with each other, with the kids and work from at home.

Get a budget billing plan, start saving for themselves and the children.

A number one priority, have life insurance and savings on everyone in the family.

Harry needed God to be in the midst of the marriage.

Sit down and talk about their problems and money.

Stop avoiding professionals who try to help them, but be open to new information.

Learn, grow and listen to the knowledge because many failed, because of a lack of knowledge.

Experience new things and do better financially.

## Story #5----Sam Carter

Sam Carter was young but he knew how to care for a family and provide. He had no kids but each woman he got intimate with had three or four children. He enjoyed working, helped clean the house, took care of the outside of the house (yard), played with the kids, was a family man and enjoyed cooking on the grill. They ate very healthy. He did so much to please the women he dated, but each time he got his heart broken. The ladies would find some sweet talker and sweep the women off their feet. That left Sam heart-broken and without a clue. He was thinking, what did he do? The women made him feel pointless. He knew he was being a man and he was. This kind of punishment make a person feel so small. Like what does he/she have that I don't? Most of the time the grass is not greener on the other side. Don't be no fool and mess up a good thing when you have it! Know what you have and keep it because times are hard out there in the world. Work smart, not hard, work together and pray together. That didn't stop Sam from moving forward; it slowed him down for a minute but he's moving.

## Sam Had to Rethink

He has a plan to marry one day. Sam isn't going to let a few rotten potatoes bring him down.

Sam has been serving the Lord and going to church, to help with his downfalls.

He now owns a business, and someday wants to have kids.

He is working on investments, retirement savings and does have life insurance. Older adults always had life insurance because they knew it was important. Even through many didn't have the right kind and definitely not enough coverage. Sam's mother did teach him that.

He wants to be stable before marriage and have everything in place.

We have to understand, in this life, no one is here to stay on earth forever. We came into this world alone and will leave alone and they both cost money. It costs to be born and when you pass away, we have to pay a price. That is something to think about.

Sam got married, years later. He had everything and his wife didn't have to work.

Story #6----Mark Muffin

A mighty man of our Lord and Savior Jesus Christ. Mark is a man who loved the Lord, the Lord has done great things in Mark's life. This man attended church daily, Monday thru Sunday. He was doing great until his wife and children started being disrespectful and wouldn't give him respect. It caused his marriage to go downhill and even separate about seven times. He would teach/preach the word of God to many but had no clue how to fix his own marriage. It got so bad, it turned him back into some of his old sinful ways and was pulling him away from God and God's word. He started sinning with his eyes, touching with his hands and using curse words out of the mouth. Doing the opposite of what God wanted him to do. (Romans 7:20), it is the sin that dwells in him.

## Mark Has Lost His Way

Mark tried to help others but didn't know how to save his own marriage.

Was he truly after God's own heart?

Mark ended up showing people the demons that were in him.

Your Bible is the basic instruction before leaving this earth. So why aren't we obeying the BIBLE?

Mark has good intentions but what about leadership?

Mark had no money being invested, no savings, no retirement plan and only his job's life insurance.

Watch your reaction when serving God. You want to become better, not worse. People are watching you. (Romans 8:6), a carnally minded person.

## Story #7---Eric Greene

Eric is a man who knows he is handsome and is a good lover. He has lots of females that are hooked on him. No one wants to let him go. Many know about the other ladies but still sleep with Eric, when he comes around. He had a few children by different ladies but that didn't stop him from getting all he can get. These females would do anything to help him, whenever Eric needed help, they would sell themselves, sell food, steal out of the store, sell their food stamps, and sell their jewelry. He cared about two of the ladies, the other ones he just used. He never worked but they loved him. They would even fight over him. They all just wanted to be loved and feel good. Eric had a funky good time; he had many to love. If one or two were mad with him, he had plenty of others in line waiting.

## Eric's Dream was Women

Eric was doing too much, and forgot about his kids.

He should have spent time with his children, instead of with all kinds of women.

He is enjoying his every moment, the feeling, because it's free.

The women allowed him to play and he took advantage of the opportunities.

The women need to wake up, because they are only getting a wet tail.

He had nothing to offer but sex, though the females call it love.

Women, is this what you want, to share a man for the rest of your life?

We all have to dream big dream and need to move on with our lives.

Mark needed to settle down.

Story #8---Donald Dickson

Donald Dickson pushed his wife's last button and she left him. Donald never really took care of his other children, the kids' mother always had them. He paid no child support, and hasn't seen them in years. Donald's wife had one child by him and she moved far away from him. Donald disrespected her many times and she told him, "I am going to leave you one day." She thought about a plan and how to take care of the little girl. She signed up for a job and checked on an apartment. She had enough money to get to work and pay rent for eight months. She felt so much better when she left and her life began to look toward the bright side of things. Donald's wife was miserable for years, but it is looking better now. It has been four years and Donald has no clue where they moved. Donald is lonely and wants them back. He's been in and out of the nuthouse. He is losing his mind. You never miss the well until it runs dry. Have respect and be kind to everyone.

Donald Didn't Take His Marriage Seriously

Donald Dickson's marriage ended and he went to counseling.

He should have shown his wife more love.

Donald took his wife for a joke. Thank God, she had a plan.

He is just realizing what he had and now it is gone.

He may never get her back.

Donald is taking it hard, and is learning from his mistakes.

He ran his wife away from him.

Story #9---Timothy Mack

Timothy has been laid off work. He always helped his wife with the children. He used to clean house, do yard work and go to the market. Until one Friday night; Nicole (his wife) stayed away from home and returned on Sunday night. He had the children and Nicole didn't call, not one time. She had started getting high three months ago. Timothy Mack had no idea but he started seeing some changes with Nicole. She stopped cooking and cleaning the house. She was shaking sometimes, and being mean when she didn't have her drug. She started lying, drinking more beer, telling people she needed food, and asking for money. But she would never give the money back to the people she owed. She would act like she had to use a family member's bathroom and ended up in their bedroom stealing. Three times she caught a cab and went to her mother's house and when she didn't have money to pay for the cab, her mom pay for it. Her mother told Nicole never to do it again because she will not pay for it. Timothy packed his bags and the kids and left her. His friend helped him find a job and he's now working again. He's taking good care of the children. He is going to court to try to get the kids for good.

Timothy is Getting Things in Order

Timothy had a plan, after the break up.

He loved his kids. He started thinking about his life and the children.

He has been going to church with his brother.

He is praying for his wife and thinking about a divorce.

He didn't understand why Nicole was asking for food and money.

He paid all the bills; food was always in the house and she was using people for her drugs.

He noticed Nicole's hair was always a mess and she wouldn't wash her clothes.

After going to court for two years, Timothy finally got custody of his children.

Story #10—James Brown

James went out with a few buddies on Saturday night. They had met a few nice attractive young ladies. They had gone to Dollies Club on Summer Street, in Pennsylvania. James was dancing with Debbie, the song came on. "Hey, let's do it, let's dance across the floor, hey, let's do, it let's dance, let's do it some more!" They were getting down! Next song was; "The Beat Goes on and the beat goes on." The last song was, "Do you want to get funky with me, do you want, ha?" After the party was over, they all exchanged phone numbers with the ladies. James knew what kind of lady he wanted to be with and this girl seemed like she was a match. As he was riding in the car, he began singing "It feels good, yeah! It feels good." James had a home, two cars, and he has his own business. He just wanted a beautiful woman for his wife. They went out about ten more times and became very close. James was singing to Debbie; "Do you like what you see? And I like what you are doing to me, don't stop what you are doing to me."

James Brown Got Married

James and Debbie got married years later and had two children.

Debbie didn't have to work but did work. She had her own Primerica business making one million a year.

They always put God first in their life and prayed.

They worked together as a team.

They invested most of their money and had their emergency savings, they would be well set for retirement and their children were straight too.

It is possible to meet your goals and make it in life. It takes two to make everything alright, it takes two, to make it out of sight.

# Curses Can Stop A Vision

◇◇◇◇◇◇◇◇◇◇◇◇◇◇◇◇◇◇◇◇◇◇◇◇◇

Most people walk through life with a mask on their face, hiding behind an act of joy but in reality, they are about to explode wide open. We are holding on to things that had been done in the past and there is no way to undo it. It happened years ago and it is now in the past. Stop looking behind you because you keep tripping and falling into your own trap. When you stay focused on the past it keeps you on lockdown and you can't focus correctly. Always mad, hurting, crying, doing evil for evil, trying to get back at a loved one and wanting others to agree with you. (Romans 12:17). Thinking it is right to hurt others because you hurt, thinking it is ok to get even, seeking revenge and most of the time people are gone on with their lives and not even thinking about you. They have been forgiven by God and moved on in life. If they are trying to talk to you and make amends, it is because it's the right things to do in the eyes of God. You have been going to church for years and can't forgive a loved one. Are you walking in darkness and refusing to forgive (1 John 1:6)?

Many of us want to hurt people, want to blame others, feeling it is fine for them to be angry for the rest of their life. The truth is that you are making yourself extremely miserable. You and the person you are angry with still have to live in this world, until it is time for them to disappear. We all are leaving this earth, remember no one is here forever, this is temporary and not eternal. We can try to destroy people all we want but the only thing that matters on this earth is what we do for our Lord and Savior Jesus Christ and nothing else. Who are you are serving, the Kingdom of God, yourself or Satan (1 John 2:4)? God knows everybody heart, what we are thinking and He sees the reaction. If you are plotting, want to pay back, keep gossiping and speaking negative of another, God knows all about it. Is this holding you back from making the kind of money you want? You don't want to pass negative curses down to the kids. If you are, you can forget about the plans God has in store for you. He will not bless that mess and that unforgiving spirit. He will not release your blessing until He thinks you are ready for the gift or what He has in store for you. (James 4:8) Draw near to God and He will draw near to you. We must put on the armor of God, cast off the works of darkness and let God's light shine.

Yes! We all have felt some kind of hurt and been through rough times but you have to get over it, you are not alone. Many males/females have been through worse pain, death of a loved one, burnt in a fire, burn scars left on the skin, raped in the past, beaten in an abusive marriage or relationship, or your friend slept with your partner, etc. Many have experienced different suffering, we don't know why, don't understand but some things happen for a reason. Are you listening to God or doing things your way and giving place to the devil? (Ephesians 4:27). We just don't know when we are next, but while waiting make sure your life is lined up with the word of God. Men/Women are upset with God but He doesn't make mistake and if you are on fire for the Savior, thirsty for Him, have a burning desire and you are showing His love and doing what the Bible commends, then you should have peace in your heart because you would know that God has them. If they were faithful to our Lord and Savior, also show God's love to neighbors and many others; you are His child. Avoid playing the blame game, adding boys/ girls to your pain, still looking for people who are hurting and feel the way you feel. Miserable people love company and hurting people hurt people. Until you forgive, your life will never change and the pain will be there as long as you allow it. No one is perfect, who else has hurt you? Have you forgiven them? How about that boyfriend/girlfriend that caused you pain, did you forgive them? We are so easy to forgive a person who we slept with us because we were so in love but what about your parents, sister, brother, aunt, neighbor and friend, etc. For the women, the men break our heart so many times but we love them to death. How many times you took them back, slept with them, cried for days, were so weak, hurt but you were still with them or talking to them. Make amends with everyone you are holding accountable for your pain or you will continue to suffer alone because others are enjoying their life.

When you sit around talking about this one person or people all the time, it's controlling you and making you turn into a monster. Many already had plenty of these monsters and skeletons in their closet, hiding behind a mask, wearing a clown face, yet the truth is they are harboring much resentment. Children may be carrying resentment, when a relative, brother, sister, dad, mom, or grandparents pass away because they are most dear to them. But that is why we have the BIBLE—Our Basic Instruction before Leaving this Earth, and we need it every bit as much as the air we breathe. It is absolutely indispensable. Don't just let it sit on the desk or table, letting dust pile up on it: read it! People go to church, never take notes, they heard the word, but it went in one ear and it goes out the other ear. Once they leave the church, they can't remember what the message was about. They went to church to say, "I did a good deed today!" They never practice what the Bible teaches and that is one reason they are struck in resentment. Some think they know the Savior but are mad with the world even though they have been in church all their lives. An unforgiving spirit people blocks their own blessing and vision. Stop getting men/women to join your pity party, getting them to follow Satan's Kingdom, dragging them down and trying to confuse others' minds because your own mind is so messed up. (3 John 1:11). You are trying to change their behavior into a mean person because you are down and heartbroken. Take your life back, seek God and His agape love. God's agape love is so powerful. Don't play church, don't act Holy, never play with God's word, and get serious with wanting God's Spirit dwelling on the inside of your body. This is serious business, and until you get real with God, you will continue to keep company with miserable friends and always want to hurt others.

We all have to answer to Jesus, so are you sure you want to see the end and what your resorts with God will be?

An unforgiving spirit strays you away from a vision. Many are bruised, wounded, scorned, and all need help. Jesus Christ is the only main help for undecided situations. Avoid pulling people into your circle and pulling them down with you. When you forgive there is so much joy, peace, calm, your body feels better and the heavy burden will be lifted up off of you like never before. It is your decision to stay in the storm or get out. You are destroying yourself and passing down generational curses to your children and family members. Curses are real, if you are always talking negative about people, accuse others for your losses, your disappointment and not obeying God's word, what do you think your kids are going to do? Look in the mirror, who are you to judge? There is only, one God and He has all the answers and all power. Male/Female, so many misunderstand the table of organization, we have all fallen short of the glory of God and we are all sinners. But, in His graciousness, God gave us tools to handle all situations. Be filled with the word which is food to the soul and be filled with His agape kind of love. The agape love is an unconditional love that never fails and it's so powerful. Get your life in order with Jesus, get a vision, life insurance, and investments because all these things are important and very few have it lined up and many ignore these four things. You need all of them in order to survive and make life much easier. Forgive everyone and get a vision. You can't focus with hatred, pride and resentment. Let it go, life is too short. There should be something in your life you want to do instead of staying hurt and starting a group with angry members.

Women and men, stop telling your kids terrifying stories about the absent parent. You are helping the children hold grudges, have low self-esteem and bad behavior. They will then pass it on to their own kids. You must have loved the person because you laid down together at some point and made human beings. God never told you that life was going to be all smooth sailing. But that when the trials come, He will always be there to give you strength and lift you up. The word strength, will help carry us through circumstances that we can't seem to fix on our own. Get your Bible—read it, live by every word, obey it, show actions of love because it's food you need daily, every minute, every hour and all day long. There will always be something to make you turn away from God, especially once you start getting too close to Him. We leave the door open with too much space and the devil whispers in your ear. (Remember that time and how your life was?) Next the raging smoke comes out of your body and you are mad all over again. Many know that the devil comes to kill, overwhelm you, stir up strife, have you thinking and doing crazy things, have you to be very disrespectful, and that is how he is able to destroy the mind. The devil doesn't like to see happy people or caring families. He enjoyed putting an end to our lives. When you leave the Kingdom of light and go back to Satan's Kingdom, in the dark, God is not pleased. When you don't get the things you want, look back at your life and look at yourself. You are your own enemy, stop making all those excuses and have males/females to agree with your bad habits. You are doing wrong in God's eyes. You need a new heart (Psalm 51:10).

# Hurting People Can Kill a Vision

Hurting people are worried, stressed out, and in a lot of pain. Many will stop eating, eat less or eat all the time. Their eating habits change and the body loses or gains weight. It takes over the mind and affects the body in many ways. It is funny how we try to lose weight, by exercising, eating right, dieting, by going to the gym and go walking. Be hurt, worried, or stressed and those pounds come off like never before. It seems like it takes forever, however, to get rid of a few pounds the right way. Has anyone experienced these things? It is so hard to do right and so easy to do wrong. So many of us enjoy doing wrong, it feels better and is just a habit we are used to. But the wages of sin, hatred, holding grudges, being mean, bitter toward others and doing evil for evil? It is death! Sin has taken control of a male/female's body, mind and their vision got blocked. You can't see well or think your way out of a miserable situation. It is strange how other males/females always lose weight when hurting while some gain weight. Both can happen, either losing weight or gaining it. We can learn something new every day by listening to positive people. Are small things of the past controlling and ruining your life? You will suffer for the rest of your life until you make amends and forgive people. Do you want to hurt for the rest of your life? No, life is too short! Making peace with the boy/girl you hate, can truly help you with your problems but you have to remove pride and stop procrastinating, keep it out of your soul. (1 Peter 3:9) says, never return evil for evil.

Family, friends and others will always bring up the past, in order to hurt someone close to them. Because they are insecure, and they are suffering. Many hate to see others do better than them. They want revenge and want you to feel their pain. (Psalm 34:14) depart from evil and do good: seek peace and pursue it. You already know they are hurting! When all they need to do is, try to talk it out with God's agape kind of love with one another. Especially if loved ones are trying to make peace with you. (Psalm 122:6) We must pray for peace for everyone. God has changed many of us and He is still working on you because He wants to use you for His glory, to help other hurting persons, and so you can have a testimony. If you never went through anything, you wouldn't know that God could fix it and turn that bitterness into a breakthrough. Why fall back into the devil's tricks/hands? Because keep on living and you will see that you need to turn to Christ or run back to Him. If you don't know Christ, try giving your life to Him. He has everything you need. If you are still talking about the same old things, past hurts and you are mad all the time, you are letting a person get the best of your heart. Give no place to the devil, meaning don't let him in your life to continue to destroy you (Ephesians 4:27). You are destroying yourself enough. God has forgiven many of them because they ask Him to! So stop adding other hurting people to your group and get it right with God. We all should be thinking about being more successful, doing better, and having dreams, goals and a vision.

Be happy for the rest of your life because time is running out. It is now 2021, and you are gathering a hate group, of others that hurt too. They need help too and none of you can help each other. You sit around and talk about the same thing over, over and over like a tape recorder. Are you tired of talking about people who once hurt you? It is a test from the devil (Revelation 2:10), he is throwing you into his prison. Have you accomplished anything from this? Trust and believe some of your so-called friends and family members are tired of hearing it, but they just agree because that's what makes you feel better for a minute. Once your gang/group of miserable people are gone, your problem is still there and you are back to square one. Crying, still blaming others, you won't take responsibility for your own action because of the pride and arrogance. You aren't more important than anyone else, we all are sinners, all have struggles, all made mistakes, did some things and said some things, lied, cheated, committed adultery, but no one is perfect. God sees us, knows what we think and dearly knows each heart. Many never experience healing from God because of unforgiving spirits.

While everyone sees the worst in you, God sees the best, the best and the best in you. There are nature person/spirit church people, who are hurting and are mad because God is working on your behalf. Now they are hurting and want to see you fall apart as well. They have gotten away from God's Kingdom, into danger. Their hearts are so troubled, despite the fact that they know the word of God. The devil has come to steal the word of God out of your heart and you don't realize it, (Luke 8:12). But like people say, even the devil can quote scriptures and disobey the Word of Jesus Christ. Why go to church, if you disobey the Word? You never change and never try to save a soul for Christ but you bring males/females to your level of evil works (1 John 3:8), he who plots evil is of the devil. Hurting human beings are pointless and you have no clue of their attitude and that they are damaging themselves. Will you ever come to your senses (2 Timothy 2:26)? It is sad, get a vision, wake up, wake up and forgive. Never let men/women stop you from a vision. You have friends/family who doesn't understand where God is leading you. But some things are just between you and God and not everyone else. We need a vision, a passion for something, a goal/dream and purpose that can get us moving ahead. It takes a lot of work. You need quiet time alone, have a focused mind, a clear mind, read plenty, study, and avoid negative things/people. Practice to become better at what you want to do while others are running around, partying, talking about you, have no vision and don't respect your career. Having a career takes most of your time, it takes work and you don't have time to focus on the negative nonsense that people think about you. There are many males/females that have nothing to do, and that is why they have so much time on their hands to sit around and talk about others. But when your mind is on God and your career, God's got your back. No one is going to take care of you but you, so let people talk, and when they stop talking, then get worried. But you are not alone.

# Double Minded Person

◇◇◇◇◇◇◇◇◇◇◇◇◇◇◇◇◇◇◇◇◇◇◇◇

A double-minded person can mess up a vision. You want to do what is right but you listen to others who steer you in the wrong direction. It pulls you away from God and back onto the dark road to destruction. The road is so dark and your eyes can't see but with a vision there is light at the end of the road. Move yourself out of the way and stop trying to correct the past because it's done and you can't change the past. Many need self-improvement, so try reading books daily because you might see your attitude in something you read. You can change you, by asking God to help change your wrong thinking pattern. You are empty, frustrated, and rude (James 1:8, 4:8). These things start in the home first and what we heard from our parents; is how we act/respond to someone we hate. You need the whole body healed from head to toe. There is no way you can impact lives, with the silence of past pain built up on the inside of you. You need a new life, new attitude and clear mind. (James 4:8), Are you helping people or destroying them? Is your mind being inundated with confusion? Many say they are going to do something only to change their mind once they get a flashback from the past. Go forward or live in the past of frustration. Being double-minded is not good because you are dismayed (worried/disappointed), things have a hold on you and it pulls you down. We all need to do better, there are areas in our life that we can improve and develop a better character for yourself.

Occupy your mind with the Bible and plenty of self-help books. If you want to see a mind transform into God's image. It will help the mind change from being double minded to looking beyond your pain and your faults. Die to sin, unforgiving spirit, and search/ask for God's mercy and grace. A mind on fire, thirsty, hungry, willing to obey the Bible and the Lord, keeps the thoughts of sin and evil thinking away. You will have no time to be stressed because you are obeying the Bible. Many never obey, mature or grow up because miserable males/females love company. Get out of the double-mindset and get help, some know where their help come from but want to be stubborn (2 Corinthians 13:1-2). They are only hurting themselves and getting deeper into the hands of Satan. The evil one takes advantage of lost, hurting souls. When you serve the Lord but then return to darkness, you did the devil a big favor and he is laughing at you. He is telling you God can't help you and thank for returning to him. Now the devil is going to beat you up and down, until you get tired of being ignorant to a lack of knowledge (God's word). The devil knew you would return back to him some day, it was just a matter of time and you are back once again. The devil knows your weakness. A double-minded person with no direction hurts others and is truly lost (James 1:8).

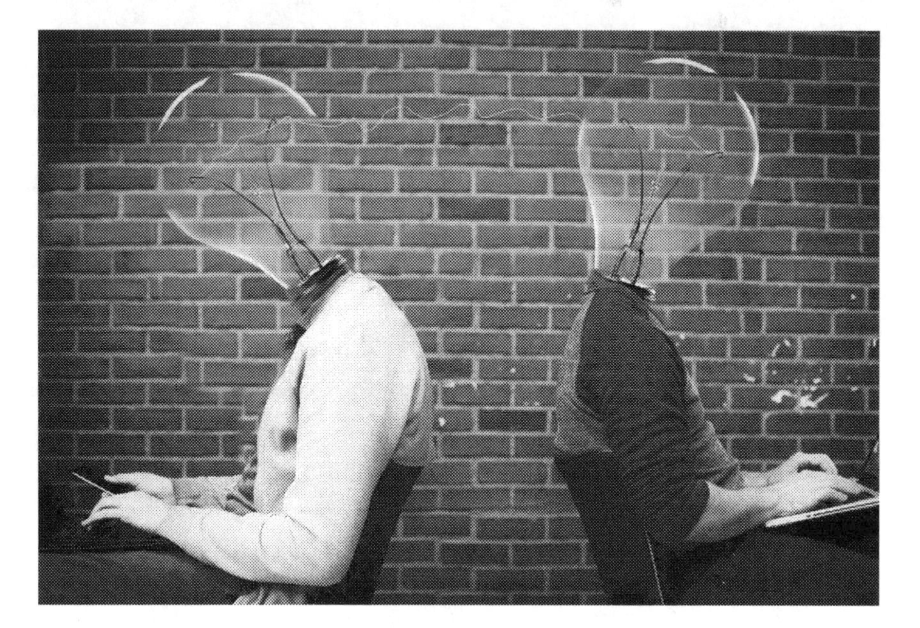

Double-minded people have blind spots and have no idea what blind spots are. It keeps them in their past pain and their eyes won't open. They just can't wake up and see the path to righteousness, everything is black to them but the road to light is at the end of the tunnel. They stop, are stuck in neutral, fall back in the pit of hell, and are weighted down with tons of bricks. Their load that they carry are so heavy, the vision is blurry, eyes can't see, they can't move and can't forgive. Resist the devil and he will flee (James 4:7). Contending with the devil's ideas are pointless. You have been taken captive by his snare, to kill and harm you. You have to deal with the blind spot because it takes over a person's life. Are you scared to deal with your blind spot face to face or head on? You are your own worst enemy. Talk things out one on one, it's not that terrible, do it and get it over but do it in love. Until you do, you will always have pain and the suffering for you will continue and never end. But you have to forgive, have a change of heart and change your mind. You have no more fuel and you need that burning desire, on fire for God and add plenty of fuel to the fire. You are dry and the fire has gone out. It will only get worse until that forgiving spirit comes forward. Other than that, Satan is having a field day with your pity parties and you stirring up envy/strife in the body. Are you tired yet of the pain, is it stopping the blessing? Some think, I'm a good person, but what kind of people are following you? Do you feel you are a leader and a good inspirational guide? Check it out in the mirror! What do you see? Does God see the best in you? Everyone should have their blind spots healed in order to get rid of the double-minded vision.

If you want to see, change the direction you are headed in because it is a trap. It's a hole in the sidewalk and you will keep falling, every time you want to commit evil acts. This is serious and you won't want to see the results coming your way. Get out of the hatred and bitterness now (2 Corinthians 10:4-6). You are confused, you have turn away from what you always believed in and the faith has faded away. You are a testimony by being your own enemy and destroying yourself as well as plenty of other males/females. Do you realize what you are putting yourself through? Get a goal and get off your high horse because you are not getting anywhere. You are losing your mind and it is a terrible thing to waste. You are wasting time dwelling on the past's feelings. You are not alone.

# Stop a Vision—Backsliders

Depressed people start falling away from God, when they have lost a loved one and blame others. They think the Word of God doesn't work but we all will be leaving here someday, so start preparing. Life is full of ups and downs, joy and pain, sunshine and rain, darkness and light, cold and hot and like a merry-go-round. Backsliders fall back when things don't seem to go their way, the way they feel it should be done or should have worked on their behalf. Next, they start accusing many others because of their heartbreak or depression (Jeremiah 5:6). Instead of appreciating life, breath in their body, roof over their head, own transportation, food on the table: they want to see what harm they can bring to another. They go off their own emotions and let the past mess them up and their focus is not clear. Moving toward destruction, hating a loved one because they are doing better. Just focusing on all the wrong things and searching for love in all the wrong persons and looking in all the wrong places. They become jealous because someone else is happy and living their dream or life. You can't stop living, when a man/woman leaves you, cheated on you, wronged you or if a dear loved one leaves the earth. It may hurt but you still have to survive on this earth until! Turning backward and into sin again, will only make things get more out of hand. (1 Corinthians 15:17) And if Christ is not risen your faith is futile: you are still in your sins. Prayer does work, when you pray the Will of the Father God and not your own words. He is an on-time God and doesn't fail. (John 6:47-48), His love is everlasting and is able to keep you from falling. God is the bread of life. Get rid of the guilt, you are born as a gift, born with greatness, be glad because of His grace and mercy. (2 Corinthians 12:9) My grace is sufficient for you, my strength is made perfect in weakness. Always look at the good times you had because they outweigh the bad days. Always count your blessings, if you are still here, have all your body parts, peace in your heart, able to move around, hear and see. These are things to be thankful for, to praise and worship the Lord. (1 Chronicles 16:34) Oh, give thanks to the Lord for He is good! For His mercy endures forever. He's wonderful every day of your life, especially if you wake up this morning, AMEN!

What a mighty God we serve. He is good all the time and would not let you down. Some feel let down but things happen for a reason. Are you faithful to God's word? Are you sharing His word? When obeying the Word of God, doing it, loving the enemy, respecting your parents/elders and winning souls to Jesus, it is a blessing. When you understand the word of God, you just can't keep it to yourself because it is like fire shut up in your bones and you have to go tell somebody else about His goodness and mercy. Are you on fire for the Lord? (Matthew 3:11) He will baptize you with the Holy Spirit and fire. Many have been going to church all your life, but haven't learned anything and have no spiritual growth. People, be very careful how you play with the Bible or play church; He sees everything we do and how we act after church. How are you going to grow spiritually if you refuse to take notes at church and not being a doer of the Word of God? When you don't serve, don't share with neighbors about Christ; go home and never pick the Bible up to read it. You need it when trials come or you will breakdown and backslide into darkness. You should focus on having more light in your life and leave that darkness out of your life (James 4:7). Make no more excuses for wanting revenge, most of the time you will continue to get hurt yourself; while plotting evil for evil (Matthew 4:1). Satan knows when you are weak; that is the best time for him to enter into your body and help you destroy yourself. (Jeremiah 3:22) If you want to be healed, you must call on God's great name. He sees you are already plotting for the big payback, revenge, I'm ready for big payback. Backsliding, do we really want to live in the past, because that is what you are doing. You are slipping and sliding into corruption, taking the body through more and more changes of pain. Get over it, grow up, be an adult and do what the Bible says to do and forgive. That is the only way you are going to heal whatever is stirring up pain and hatred. Let it go!

# WOMEN WHO ARE DEPRESSED

◇◇◇◇◇◇◇◇◇◇◇◇◇◇◇◇◇◇◇◇◇◇◇◇◇◇

Women, are you tried of being depressed? (1 Peter 5:7) "Casting all your anxieties on him, because he cares for you." Have you been with a man/ boy for years and they keep cheating, lying, act worse than a woman? Does he like to argue about small things, jealous of you because you are attractive, or they did something to hurt you and you did the same to him? You took the man back and gave them chance after chance. But that man/boy couldn't take what he dished out and he got mad. He likes throwing things up in your face about the past. He's not thinking about all the dirt he did and you let him slide. Especially if you both had children by someone else while you were apart. A man can't handle that but a woman can. Maybe he was sleeping around and you did the same. Maybe he slept with your best friend and you married his cousin and had a baby with his cousin. Men can't handle things like a woman can; we are strong in a lot of ways. Ask the man, can he stand the rain, no pressure, no pressure from you, baby. You know he needs you! He wants you and he can't live without you. Storms will come, ladies, but hang in there and be strong. Women are the weak vessel but all that pain can make us stronger. We cried, turned all night, had to be strong for the children, take care of our kids, we were left with all the bills, almost lost our mind, felt we just couldn't live without that man, took him back so many times and we still got the same results. He still hurt you again and took your love again for granted. After all you have done for him, waited patiently for him, still cared for him, still showed your love him and never turned your back on him. And if you did turn away from him; you were praying it would help him, get his life in order. We go through so much with a man that we love and they hurt us over and over. God wants us to come to Him. (Matthew 11:28), "Come to me, all who labor and are heavy laden and I will give you rest." We think to ourself, you make me feel brand new; once you take them back. You love him so much all you can think of is that he gave good love. The men tell you, I want to start a new relationship with you and should they tell their lady bye-bye. They tell you that, they want to be with you. Every woman deserves a good man, who can love her the way she loves and cares for him. Who wants to cry, worry, be unhappy, and fight every day over something petty? Fighting can cause a man or woman to hurt or kill, the one they truly love. Love can make people do crazy, crazy things. But that's the way love goes! Build yourself up because you are the finest he ever knew. Remember, (Philippians 4:13) "I can do all things through Christ who strengthens me."

The men know when they mess up because they can't find another love like yours and all the good that came with it. It takes a fool to learn that love don't love no body. They come to you with, "I want to be your man, let me love you down, I just want to be a good man, good man." Some will say, "When will I see you again; your sweet love, when will I see you again?" Try to stay away and let them know what they had because some of them just keep messing up. (Proverb 3:5-6) "Trust in the Lord with all your heart, and do not lean on your own understanding. In all your ways acknowledge him, and he will make straight your paths." You can't keep letting men keep running back and forward into your life. They keep running because of their wrongdoings. Watch out for the men who sleep around because the Coronavirus does not have a name on it, until you get it. A man will start confusing you ladies because they are doing things on purpose that they don't have any business doing that. They want you to put them out for some days so they go out in the streets to fool around. You keep letting them back in, how can you explain yourself for letting them back in? Next, you are back in love again, back in love. You think, you can't be with anyone else. You shouldn't rush being with another; take your time. Take your time and do it right. It's ok to be single for a while. (Matthew 6:33) "But seek first the kingdom of God and his righteousness, and all these things will be added to you."

When other men see you walking down the street, and they are watching, ladies, they will be asking you: are you single, are you single? They've been looking at you for quite a while and you've been on their mind every day and every night. The things you do and said, seem so outstanding that other men just love you. You know it is not working with you and your man. They make it seem like they love you but they keep hurting you. It seems like they love you and it is crazy because love is caring. You must create a backup plan for your life and for your children, if you don't have one already. Don't ever wonder, you are the highest of the high. Have a vision and live your dreams. Men will come and try you again. They ask, can I talk to you for a minute? The men tell you, "Honey, honey, you put my love on top, who-come on, baby; you drive me crazy." Let the wind hit your face and turn that love in another direction. Fly high and spread your wings, like a bird up in the sky. Men tell you that you are the one he loves; you are the one he needs and the one he sees. He tells you that you are the only one that he calls and you are the only one that can fulfill his needs. The women say, if it isn't love, why does he stay on my mind and make me feel so sad inside. If it isn't love, why does it hurt so bad and make me feel so sad inside? Many women just can't let go of that feeling. Just as much as he is on your mind, you are on his mind and his heart is shattered in a thousand pieces as well. Love doesn't hurt or cause pain.

Women, you rock their world but men try to play their hurt off. Men cry too; they cry in the dark. But God is there for all women who are in pain and are hurting. God is here, to help dry up those tears and love us the way we should be loved. Put Him first and He will give you love. You need a gentleman that wants to give you everything, give you the world and love you the right way. You want to be loved by a man after God's own heart! Who knows how to treat and take care of a good woman! Stop giving attention to what you don't have because God can't work with what you don't have. Things that cause you pain, stop your vision, hold you back and a man who pulls you down. Pray about your sorrow and He can work with that. If a man left you or keeps running in/out of your life, let God build you up, turn things around, heal you and give you living water, flowing in and through you. Men can stop your focus; a negative man lives in the natural mind and knows nothing about God, nor does he understand a spiritual mind. Many men don't know how to truly love a woman. Many men never had a love like yours and can't handle a warm--hearted woman. They can't handle a virtuous woman, for her price is far above rubies (Proverbs 31: 10-31). A virtuous woman, she opens her mouth with wisdom, and in her tongue is the law of kindness. She is worth more than silver and gold. She is kind/gentle and does him good. If you serve God and your partner doesn't, you are unequally yoked. Meaning you both are not on the same path and are not headed in the same direction. Try not to think like the world, follow Jesus Christ, not the world. Focus on what you have and what God has already done in your life. If you are in good health, your mind is clear, your kids are fine, you have a home, a roof over your head, all your body parts, food on your table, eyes that can see, you can feel, are able to talk and walk; thank God! That is enough right there. Praise Him for the little things you have and have faith as small as a mustard seed and maybe then He will give you more. But you have to acknowledge the little things you have.

Go somewhere in your home, close the door and pray. Women get struck on these men and it stops them from thinking positive things. Take your mind off of the problem. God is God, God is love, a healer, a way maker, a doctor, He is everything you need and the only thing you need. When you accept Jesus into your heart, trouble doesn't last always. If there wasn't a devil you wouldn't have a chance to grow. The devil is real and so is Almighty Jesus Christ. If you never had a problem, you would not know that God could fix it. All things are possible to them who believe in our Lord and Savior Jesus Christ. Take yourself out of the problem and let God do what He needs to do. He doesn't need you to help Him. He will take care of your husband/boyfriend, you just keep that person in prayer. They need God, we all do and He wants us to come to Him for help and a vision. Avoid being caught up in your feelings, so God can move in your life. Feelings, so deep in your feelings, feelings help you need a healing and get over your feelings. Feelings help you become stronger and get over your fear. Then you will see yourself peeling away from that man who hurt your feelings; that is when you start becoming better and can focus on what is really important in your life and what is best for the children if you have any. That man is standing in your way, hindering your view, crippling the mind, weakening your soul, and blocking your big dream. I know you really wanted it to work, but some people and things are only in our lives for a season and to make us stronger. To overcome this feeling, you will need Jesus Christ's help to lead you on the right path of an abundant life. Jesus is our Shepherd! (John 10;10) The thief does not come except to steal, and kill, and to destroy; I have come that they may have life and that they may have it more abundantly. That is better than being disrespectful, unappreciated, unloved and someone who doesn't deserve a queen. Stop taking care of these men, women have been doing this for far too long. Look how they treat you and disrespect you. That means they don't appreciate all the things you have done for them. You know in your heart you have turned over backwards for these men and they still treat you badly. You can't even think straight. He's in your way and you can't see your dream. You know you can do better for yourself. Do you like being stressed and worried all the time? We all deserve a king who truly is after the Lord's own heart; not a worldly man that doesn't know how to love a queen.

There are some women who have turned to drugs, prostitution, dancing in clubs, sleeping with different men all the time, have low self-esteem, stop caring about how they look, bad words always come out of their mouth, and they don't know how to treat a good man when they come to you. Just because one or a couple of men mistreated you, there are still a few good men out there; it might not be that many but be patient and stop settling for anything or for less. Your body is a temple of God, (1 Corinthians 3:16). Do you not know that your body is a temple of God and that the Spirit of God dwells in you? You don't have to move to fast because you are hurting. You are not the only one, there are plenty of women who go through the same things but different hurts, different abuse, but they all are suffering in some kind of way. But if you want a better lover, better life, better leader, a man who listens, a man that understands, and who loves you for who you are, we have to let go of all the trash that is in the way. We are sinking, soaking in our own body. Dry those eyes and stand tall. Glorify God, praise Him, Honor God, Worship Him in body and Spirit. (1 Corinthians 6:19). Or do you not know that your body is the temple of the Holy Spirit who is in you, whom you have from God, and you are not your own. Everything in this world belongs to God. Stop putting your body through so much mess, it's not worth it; you are destroying/killing yourself. If you have children, they need you. Many are harming themselves, murdering the kids too, and that isn't fair. Be careful if a man puts his hands on you, don't allow that because it can get really dangerous and end up in death. God doesn't want you living in that type of relationship. You need a man who encourages you and you both build each other up in love. Read (1 Thessalonians 5:11, 4:4) God can't send you what you need, with that rotten banana (man) in your presence. You must pray for Him to remove that man and He will do just that!

When you let these devils back and forward in your life, most of the time it gets worse because Jesus is not present in their life. When they come back, they bring plenty of more demons with them and they are all in your home laughing at you. New devil, more problems, more pain and it is just a new level of hurt. He does right for some days, then the man starts stabbing you in the back again, and the demons stay longer and longer. Be careful when taking men back, especially if he is putting his hands on you. Don't make that last time, be your last time here on earth because it happened too many times. Be aware of the signs and say no; don't go because it can depend on life or death. It could be a trick or setup; tell him to keep that sweet talk to himself. (Ephesians 4:26-27) Be angry and do not sin, do not let the sun go down on your wrath. Don't give place to the devil. You fell for it again, not knowing what God has for you is only for you. He has a purpose, vision, and plan in place for you. (James 4:7) "Therefore submit to God. Resist the devil and he will flee from you." How many of us have gotten saved and belong to God's Kingdom now and people have left you alone but they will tempt you? And try to get you to fall back into your old habits. Some women have left God and try to be a bad girl, just to keep a relationship with that man they love or called it love. And the man still disrespecting that woman. They make you feel so small and small-minded. A man should be kind to you. (Read Ephesians 5:21). Get your life and house in order. No one knows the day or time when Jesus will come (Matthew 24:42) Watch therefore, for you do not know what hour your Lord is coming. Be careful of the things you do and how you spend your time. Time is short and is running out; you have no time to stay stuck in a miserable marriage or relationship.

If something is beating you up and down, ask God to step in and help you. Pray for what you don't want; if you don't want pain and bitterness, pray about the circumstances. Stop thinking about someone who is not treating you like the queen that you are. Where your mind goes, the body follows it! If you are focusing on that no good person and you are following them or staying stuck worrying about him. When you gave good, good love, cooked, clean house and he doesn't realize he needs to change, waiting for him to change, it is not going to happen. Only God can and will change a person if you come to Him and ask. God is supernatural and can do anything but fail. Avoid being locked down, in jail, in a deep hole, living in a box, crying in the bed or corner. You will be depressed and cry but we all have to get up and keep pushing, keep on pushing, to the hill where our help comes from the Lord. Miracles will never happen on what you want and what you don't have. Success is not by accident! It will come with the little that you have and thanking God for it. Use the little He gave you, don't complain because it can and will take that little bit from you. Just be thankful for what you've got! You may not have a great big house, expensive diamonds, big nice car, a husband, or all the money you need; not yet. God perhaps can't trust you with some of these things right now because you are not using the little things He gave you. You might not be serving Him, the way you should and not doing what He told you to do. He is waiting on you to make that move that He has been trying to show you and you are missing it every time. He is speaking to you and trying to show you what is wrong with this picture. You have to get the big picture or you will continue to be lost in worldly things and what you want. It is not a need, if God didn't give it to you; it is what you want and can't let go. Until you do you will continue to stay on that same merry go round and keep going in circles like a spinning top. Spinning, spinning, spinning, going around and around, and refusing to get help to get out of the relationship. It's like you are in the middle of a tennis court and the ball keeps hitting you in the head and knocking you down. The man sweet talks you and you are back in his arms again -- until the next heart ache. Next you are in more pain than before. So sad, that we let one person drag us down, to where we can't even think. Wake up, wake up; it is time to move, so get up and dance your pain away, you've got a problem and need to dance that pain away.

There are men/women who try to steal your joy. Afraid to see you happy and doing good. Try to find a man who doesn't live in the darkness, has wisdom, has a loving heart and caring spirit because a dead man can't feel your pain. All he does is repeat himself by hurting you, over and over. You are trying to figure out why this man wants you upset and out of your mind. "When all I do is love him and do right by him." Most of us just want to be loved and be happy, but it is always the one you love so much. We have to let them go, be still, move on and love that man from a distance. Troubles don't last forever; storms may come this we know but can you stand the rain? That man will have to clean up what he messed up while you are starting your life all over again. Most men will not get that queen back because when a woman is fed up there is nothing that man can do about it. Just like the wind blows and no one can stop it; you need to fly away and never go back to him. Nothing can stop a hurricane, a rainstorm, a tornado, you can't stop the sun from shining, you can't stop the moon, you can't stop thunder and lightning, the stars or the snow and death can't stop the wind. The wind is invisible and there is no way you can hold it back. Let nothing hold you back from your dreams, time to get a new start, get in the wind, new mindset, a new heart, new change, new personality, new tongue, and a new life no matter how upset you were. Have the power of God's Spirit, let God's wind blow you and help turn your life toward the Holy Spirit. Let the wind of God blow you and carry you to a place you never been before. God is so faithful, so loving, so powerful and we all need the fire of God dwelling on the inside of us. Refuse to let the wrong wind blow you in the wrong direction. If that man doesn't know how to honor you, tell him to move out of your way. Because help is on the way for you and it will be a wind of a hurricane or tornado that will move him, if he needs help. God got your back, as long as you ask Him, accept Him into your life and He will cover you with His wings. Life is a precious gift from God and you have no more time to waste on pain and hurt. Get over it, get out and fly like an eagle to the sea; fly like an eagle let your spirit carry me. Is the wind blowing in your life and taking you to that secret place where you shine and have a clear mind?

It is love that makes a woman. Yes, it's love that makes a woman. Women in leadership build up other women, young ladies and teach them the ins and outs. Some men will come into a lady's life, knowing they are married and won't tell you. But what they will tell you is; if loving you is wrong, I don't want to do right. You have to reject that offer, let them know it is cheaper to keep her (his wife). Start teaching your girls how to respect their bodies, be a woman of God, take their time with wanting a man, and guard their hearts. Tell your sons to be gentlemen, love a lady the way a man should love their mom, and have a goal, so, if he ever wants to marry, he will be financially stable and ready to care for himself and his family. No one is perfect and you will get hurt, just try to let your children know how life can be and prepare them for the world. Women have to be stronger. We feel that we have to belong to them (a man) and that we should be together with them as one and forever. When a male hurts a woman, we fall apart and we feel we have lost a part of ourselves. "We belong together, baby; when you left, I lost a part of me and I am falling apart. Come back, baby!" The man will come back when he feels like it because he knew you would wait, no matter how long he decides to stay away. Leave that man alone and let it rain on him. See if he can stand the rain, the pressure, the storm while in the rain. Let him taste his own medicine. See if he still wants to be your man. Let these men come back to you begging, saying, "I want to be your man, I want to be your man." Or I like when we play the kissing game, it is such a good thing; and I never felt so good. I like the way you kiss me, baby; when we play the kissing game. Give him something to think about. While you are out dancing, to the song; to do me, baby, do me, baby.

Avoid letting a man see that you can't live without him, or that you can never love anyone else. We know it's hard to let go and hard to say good-bye to yesterday. Is he worth you losing your mind, be constantly worried, stressed out and losing weight? Some women gain weight from a miserable relationship. Women, do you remember a time in your life where you were exercising, trying to get your body in shape or wanted to lose weight and it wasn't working fast enough? How many of us experienced a bad relationship and that weight disappeared right away? That's a hell of a way to lose weight, but it's true. People gain weight when they are in a happy relationship and things are going well. What do you think is better for the body, exercising or a heathy relationship? Stop letting these terrible relationships hold you back from a vision or something great. Don't let an abusive man make a mistake and make you take your last breath here on earth. We see, we hear and have experienced these things on TV, in the world, movies, in marriage and people in the family. Be aware of the signs that can cause life or death. Find a better man or lover. Let the man/boy come to you saying I can't live without you, that he is not happy when you and him are not close to one another and that it just hurts him so bad. That it makes him want you more and that he wants you so bad. Do me, baby, like you never done before; I just want you so bad. Believe it or not, men can't live without women.

Have him thinking, when will I see you again; when will I see you again? I just want to be a good man; good man. Then you can tell him, sorry, you're not my kind, you're not my, you're not my kind; O no! Tell that man, I used to be your girl but you disrespected me and I moved on. I used to be your girl and I respected you, when you were my man and I never neglected you. So, I'm not going to give you another chance because I gave you the world, my soul, and everything that was in me. You just hurt me so bad; all I needed was a shoulder to cry on and you left me there standing alone. I always wanted to be down with you, just wanted to be down, down and you made me look like a clown. Now I'm going to dance my pain away, no more problems; dance my pain away and no more pain. Let him know you are going to fly like an eagle to the sea, fly like an eagle and let God's spirit carry me. I'm going to find that man, I don't care what you say; I'm going to find him and his name is Jesus Christ. Let him know, you want to be alone but with somebody else. You want to be alone but with Jesus Christ. It is not going to be anymore half-stepping, no more half-stepping because it's about that time for a change and have a peace of mind. When you change, make up in your mind that it's all over now. The man will try to figure you out and wonder how you got where you are. God can make you feel brand new but you have to give Him a chance. Sing to yourself; you make me feel brand new, I sing this song to you, Lord. You make me feel brand new. Let that man see you are doing fine without him and that it is nice to be alone and have a peace of mind. It must be nice coming into the arms of your Lord and Savior.

# Men Hurting Women

Wake up, mighty men, and get a vision. Are you still lying to women, hurting them for no reason? You know they love you very much; is that why you hurt them and you know they will always take you back? Many men were raised up without their father but that gives you no right to mistreat a lady. That is why the Bible, Holy Spirit and Jesus Christ is here to guide us all. Does that make you feel like a real or big man when you hurt the one you love? Or do you really love her? Are you jealous of your woman? She is with you and loves you. If she didn't love you, she wouldn't waste her time on you. You are stopping your vision and can stop her dreams/goals; she is there to work side by side with you. Did you not know that she is your helper? You want to be loved and so does a lady; we all want to be loved. But God has that love that we all are searching for. Look to Him to make you a wise man or husband; that is what your lady needs in her life. When you find God's love and know who you are in Jesus Christ, that is when you can love that woman the way she should be loved. She doesn't want to suffer every day; with a man she truly loves, it should be peace in your home, not destruction. Men do things and blame it on drinking. "I've been drinking, I've been drinking," and they couldn't keep their eyes off of other women and failed for temptation. A wise man makes wise decisions; they have a vison and make no excuses about why they can't love their lady like they should. Love is kind, sweet, showing you care, patient, being partners, talking together, laugh/cry together, work together, speak the truth in love, and love unconditionally. God's agape kind of love which loves no matter what happens or what you are going through. God may be missing in your life. Let God challenge you to be a better man; if it doesn't challenge you, it doesn't change you. Try God, try faith. It can move mountains.

Some men never apologize to their lady, for hurting them over and over again. They never realize that they are broken. Have you ever through about why you haven't changed and keep hurting the woman you love? Grow in all the fruits of the Spirit. All these fruits are good for you and the woman's soul. It will help you have a healthy relationship. You must be aware of what you think, accept what you have, make her feel like a queen and never argue in front of children. When you hurt the woman, the children see it and they hurt because their mom is hurt and cries. Do you not know that when you are hurting her, the children hurt and suffer too? Let them see you are a loving dad, good husband and a caring person. Is that hard to do, or do you like ladies to go through pain? When they have your children, you don't think that is enough pain for her? If you think you can change, you can do it. (Proverbs 23:7) For as he thinks in his heart, so is he. A man/woman wouldn't change because they like the sin in their lives. They enjoy other females and how they make him feel (King) so they can't stop cheating. They don't know how to change and love her; it is that pride in you, as a man. A goal, dream and vision demand a change, and that is precisely why many people don't care to have one. It will make a person's life greater and better. Grow up and be a role model for other men and for your sons. You shouldn't want them to treat women like you do. Would you want someone to run over the top of your mother and mistreat her? Treat women the way you want to see your mom in a marriage or relationship. It starts with you, a change in your own life. Learn to love yourself first and you will be able to love that queen and the children. Avoid the worldly things that you see other guys do, especially if they are harming their women and kids. Believe you can change, and then change, you have a choice and a chance to start now.

You men know the women love you and care for you. They comfort you and try to talk to you but refuse to listen. You know they will come when you call because they love you. Now you both have to go your separate ways; you did her wrong and were unfaithful. You have to clean up what you messed up and start all over again. How would you feel if the woman you loved did the things you did to her? Put yourself in a woman's shoes and let us see you wear them. If you know what I mean. You wouldn't like it; most of the time the grass is not greener on the other side. And the other women can't do you like she can, or treat you the way she did. You know you love that lady more than anything in this world besides your kids that you had by her. You don't deserve her, she's got to find her another lover in those jeans. You are guilty of loving other women. Guilty because she is leaving you because you refuse to do right by her side. Guilt is a major problem; you need God's grace and His love. You have to learn to put that woman first but you forgot to be her lover. The fights start getting worse after all that she has done for you. Put that woman first because she can play too, but a good woman doesn't have to flaunt her body. She avoids sleeping around just because you sleep around. If you love her, say it, show it, do it and prove it. Your problem isn't sin; it is sickness. But you are not alone.

Many will not change their behavior but will change their belief system. You must change that behavior and think different. You don't have guilt because you see nothing wrong with lying and cheating. You don't see anything wrong with a little bump and grind. You don't see anything wrong with pulling people down every time they get back up. But she will find someone to love and care for her. And she will be back in love again! Messing with temptation will get you in trouble. It'll break up your happy home. Even with Coronavirus going on, some people still won't change. Just keep making the one you love miserable. It's up to that person who keeps taking you back or to set you free. She will find someone to tell her something good and tell her they love her. It will be like a dream come true for her. Someone that can have that key to her heart, back at square one and they will become one. You will be getting on your knees, missing her, wanting her because you may never see her again. She will exhale, move on, laugh, cry tears of joy because life never tells us why these things happen. She will find someone that she prayed for all her life. Another man might come sweep her away and turn her life around. Next, she will be thanking God for that good man. You better treat her like a lady, before someone else loves her the way you can't. It will be too late to talk for a minute. You men will be singing, "nothing from nothing leave nothing; you got to have something if you want to be with me." You are unhappy because you wanted to play and now, she is gone. You now have to clean up, your mess and start your life all over again. You will never find another love like that again. You had your helpmate but took her for granted.

Men, what do you do when you love somebody? And everything is going wrong. Here you go again, woo wo woo, baby, here you go again. You keep running back to me again. I thought what we had was over now. Men, why do you lie, cheat, hurt them? Do you truly love that woman? You know many women would do anything to keep a man they love. They don't want to share you in the bed with someone else because she wants you all to herself. Not in between the sheets with other females. I'll do anything for you, I'll do anything for you and I hope very soon you see all that love she has for you. Do you think it is time to go your separate ways and let it burn, let it burn? It takes a fool to learn that love don't love nobody. You make her feel like a fool in love. While you are out there in the streets watching ladies, go by watching ladies, go by watching them. Knowing you got a woman at home sweet as can be, a woman who cares about you, she's over the hills for you and deeply cherishes you. You have a woman on the outside crazy about you. You are walking down the street watching ladies, in and out of love with the one who loves you with all her heart. Shame, Shame, Shame, Shame on you as a man! That's what some of you men do; can't wait for summer to watch the ladies. Summer, summertime, everything is going be alright, it's going to be alright! You got a woman at home sweet as can be, a woman on the outside crazy about you, when you are trying to love two; it is not easy to do. You need someone, somebody to help you turn your life around; you need a hotshot. She doesn't want to hear you been drunken, you been drunken; blaming it on the goose, blaming it on Crown Royal, blaming it on beer and blaming your buddy. Is it worth taking your eyes off of the woman who was by your side through thick and thin and putting your eyes, on another lady? What's love got to do with it; what's love got to do with it? It has everything to do with it, when you love somebody. And everything is going alright; here we go again; here we go again and you keep coming back again. If you had one wish and wishes came true, which woman would you wish for? A woman to spend your whole life with, to make that dream come true. Falling in love is so easy to do but getting out of a relationship, for a woman, is hard. Men, if you can't stop messing around, can't control yourself, maybe you should stay single. You must stop telling these women you want to know their names. You wonder if you take them home, will they make love to you and you want to be their man. And that you are living a single, single, single life when you have a lady/wife at home. Try having a vision, settle down, take your time, love yourself, and later find the woman of your dreams. Let's chill, let's settle down, that's what you should be doing. Just you and her, chilling, settling down, marriage and last kids.

Treat her like a lady, treat her like a lady, when you love somebody, never give her up but treat her like a lady. You should never give up on a good thing, never give up on that good thing and never give up on her good loving. Never give up on that thing called love. Admit when you have a problem, talk to each other and see if you both can get to the root of the problem. Men, you have to express yourself, express yourself and believe, express, believe; just express yourself. You must believe in your mind that you can be that gentleman she needs you to be, the great dad or husband someday. Be the man/king she wants to spend the rest of her life with, she wants you. We all want to be loved and you are not alone. Tell her something good, tell her that you love her, yeah; tell her something good. Make it last forever, make it last forever, she wants to be your girl, think about that main lady who you really adore. The one that holds all the keys to your heart and always opens the door to take you in when you were down and out. Did you forget all the good deeds she has done for you and sacrificed her love for you (Hebrews 13:15), (Psalm 40:6)? The fruit of her lips still loves you and shows she cares, every time you needed help. It takes two, to make everything go right, it takes two, to make it out of sight and the beat goes on and the beat goes on. Two hearts full of love, joy, peace and patience, will fill a house with blessings/happiness. That is what many people want in the world today. God's agape kind of loves makes all the difference in a person's heart. When you've been through so many bad situations in life, hang in there and please don't fail that woman now. She is your helpmate, your best friend, your children's mom, and your partner. You will never find another love like hers, never find another love like this again or a warm heart like hers.

You know you love that woman; I don't care what you say, you love her, you love her; she really loved you and she makes you feel brand new every day of your life. She would do anything for you and you need to do the same for her. Men, tell the woman you love her and mean it. I'll do anything for you, I'll do anything for you, and that you hope very soon she sees all the love you have for her because you have been holding so much love inside because you thought it was too much for her. Trust and believe she wants all the love you have for her. Women give all their love and they want you to give all of your love to them. Men, you don't want to be singing, she used to be my girl, she used to be my girl; I reject her, didn't respect her and now she is gone. You will be holding back the tears of time; from all those years of ups and down. Men, you will regret losing that woman, singing, I'm lost without you and I'm hurting inside. This pain can stop men/women from a vision and getting ahead because of your wrongdoing. Get a vision together, make it work and make it last for a lifetime. Let your love for one another shine, smile and let others say, "it must be nice, must be nice." It is a beautiful thing when two people's hearts are filled with love for each other. She just wants you to be her candy man and she will be your sweet potato pie. When you both can smile, you both can say, "it must be nice." Taking each other back down memory lane, taking each other to love land, baby, love land. Men, show and tell her that you feel the same way she feels. Show and tell, that a game we play, when you want to say, "I love you." Boy, so show her and tell her that you feel the same way she feels. Being miserable is a hurting feeling and blocks people vision. Sometimes we laugh, sometimes we cry, but life never tell us the reason why! If you love someone, build them up and never knock them down.

Men, God forbid, if something happens to that lady that you love. How would you feel? You won't be able to run back to her anymore. You won't be able to treat her wrong for no reason. You are going to miss her sweet love, her warm touch, her ear to listen, and her smooth lips. You are going to remember all the fights you picked with her, you putting your hands on her and all the pain you caused her. Knowing she didn't deserve any of that; she stood by your side, took you back, took up for you, gave you true real love, did anything for you and for what or why did you hurt her so bad? You break up and make up, you mess up and all of a sudden you want her back. You are the man of the house and you should be lifting your lady up. Work with her on a business and become successful. If you start a business and she sees you are doing a great job and making money, guess what, she will follow you. As long as it's righteous in God's eyes. She doesn't want to fight and argue; women just want some of your time, a trustworthy relationship, a faithful man and plenty of love. It makes a person feel really good to know they are loved, have a faithful man and someone who cares. When you hurt them for no reason, it can keep them away from doing great things in their life, as well as for their children. Please build the women up and let them see you as a man doing great things for them, your kids, and others. Avoid fronting in front of friends, at church, work, family, social media, Facebook, Instagram etc. When you are behind closed doors beating on your woman like scrambled eggs and beating her like a punching bag. Just remember, kids now will get you back someday for hurting their mom. If they know their mom is beautiful inside out and is very loving. Please have respect for the woman that loves you very much and respect the children too. Children love their parents. Don't destroy her, love her; don't hurt her, support her; and don't let her sink but help her swim. Never put your hands on your woman. Accidents do happen but the wrong accident can happen which can cost her life and yours. Something that could have been prevented. Avoid hurting the one you love. If your mind isn't right, get help or think about your own mother. You wouldn't harm your mother, would you? Don't do something you will regret. You are not alone.

LEADERSHIP

# Be a Leader and not a Follower of Destruction

◇◇◇◇◇◇◇◇◇◇◇◇◇◇◇◇◇◇◇◇◇◇◇◇◇

Let's impact other's lives by showing leadership. A leader shows a positive reaction and has a nice attitude. Who are you leading into God's Kingdom, or are you turning people away from God? Are many following you, is it in a bad way or with good intentions? If it's bad, your Savior is not pleased with you. Most of the hardship, pain and struggle you are experiencing is only a test of your faith (Revelation 2:10). To see if it will break you or make you stronger. Children of God, we must keep His word alive, lead others to Him and respect the Bible. You are blocking your vision and blackening your view. Everything belongs to God; He is in control; he created heaven and earth. He can do whatever He pleases to do, He can wash away the sinful world and all this hatred. Respect His commands, love one another, do a good deed for someone because you don't know who needs encouraging words. Help lift up family members and friends because this is what you learn in church and not hatred. Others are in a depressed mode too but they aren't trying to do mean thing to their enemy or persons who once caused them sorrow. It steals your joy and stops a vision. Do you want to be a leader who destroys a person because something made you angry? God is the judge and not you. Turn from your wicked ways and turn to God. He wants to shape and mode you into His image. Maybe you don't fully understand what the Bible teaches because you are disobeying it and not listening (1 John 3:8).

Maybe you are leaning to your own understanding and going by how you feel (Proverbs 3:5). Lead not unto your own understanding but let the King lead you. Never take your eyes off of the prize or off of the one person who gives you strength from day to day! God is still awesome, still the ruler, the King of the world, and healer. Are you threatening to hurt, get even, gathering hurting people to join your pain and making them miserable with you? If you are, it's a big sin (Psalm 51:4). Acknowledge the word of God because you will be judged. Jesus Christ is the only one you can trust and give your heart to, when the heart is troubled. Many of us can help males/females by sharing what we learned when we were going through a rough time in our own life and how we survived. Get it right in your heart because God's thoughts are not our thoughts, His ways are not our ways because He is way bigger than our situations (Isaiah 55:8, 9). Lean not unto your own understanding but be delivered, be set free from sin and never look back. You are perishing away, without a dream, without peace and a vision. WAKE UP, WAKE UP! Live your life peacefully with all men and stop letting sin control you. You can experience favor with God but your heart is cold and is carries a lot of pain. True, faithful children of God, understand His word, live by it, feed the body daily with the word, and know how to carry heavy burdens. Can you handle trouble and storms? If not, that is why Jesus Christ is available 24/7. He wants you to smile, laugh, feel free of problems and praise God no matter what and love unconditionally (agape kind of love). That is how a leader should lead and not pull others down with them. You want to be a blessing and not a destroyer. We all are worth something and if you believe you are; start forgiving, make amends and you will get better results. Be a leader of forgiveness.

Leadership is not a game or joke. Leadership helps with a vision and guides in the right direction. Leadership is not a contest, no one is better than anyone else and it is not competitive. Please avoid comparing yourself with others because what God has for you, it is for you and no one else. Behaving unwisely weakens the brain, weakens the body and makes a person behave unwisely (2 Corinthians 10:12-18). Die to self, lean not unto your own understanding, get knowledge of who you are, who you belong to and where you are going because anger and evildoers will be cut off (Psalm 37:8-9). To become a leader, you will have to forget some things and reach for your vision. "Forgetting those things which are behind," and reaching for a dream, goal or vision which are before you. (Philippians 3:13-15). Keep on pushing/pressing toward that goal or vision. You've been hurting too long and nothing has changed and it doesn't feel good. It will bring happiness to the remembrance, once you let go of all that junk in the trunk. If you keep being angry/ evil, God will reveal it to you because He doesn't like evil acts. Men/ Women have lost our way, lost our vision, because they never obey the word of God for years. They just went to church for their own purpose and not to change. Check yourself, check your attitude; because when

God brings correction, He don't want any excuses. You've had plenty of time to get yourself together and stop pulling others down with you.

As a leader be careful what comes out of the mouth. The tongue defiles a person. Are you speaking truth and in love? People fall away from God because they have no vision and where there is no vision, the people lack knowledge, start sinning and perish. (Proverbs 29:18). A vision is for your future. Instead of being a troublemaker, get a vision, seek the kingdom of God first and you will see things will fall in place. Stop being mad with the world, while being tempted by Satan. We know it hurt but you have the Bible, to help you along the way. Remove bearing false information about God, you go to church but are talking bad about people, can't forgive, sending mixed information to others, you love God or the devil because it can't be both (Luke 18:20). You are confusing yourself and many others with whom you keep company. They can see you are torn apart and bitter. Is that how you want to represent the Lord and Savior Jesus Christ? You feel you should be mad and have that right. The sinful ways of a man seem right but the end is death. Where is the motivation in your life? When you have no vision, Satan comes and help you find things to do and they are not good intentions but evil. Why do you keep letting Satan come back into your life? You need to take back everything the devil stole from you. Honor your father and mother because that is how you entered into this world. We say bad things about the absent parent but it is not good. A mature parent won't teach their children to disrespect the absent parent because no one is perfect.

We all came into this world alone and we all will leave this earth alone. We brought nothing with us when we came and will leave with nothing. Everything belongs to God, the Creator of the world. Be a leader, you have a testimony that can help other people but stop playing the blame game. God is not going to want to hear that because you can't do what He has called you to do because you are holding on to grudges which are crippling the body and mind. Meditate on the word of GOD and get back up, you can get back up again, get back up again because there is Power in the name of Jesus (1 Timothy 4:15). What is God telling you to do? "Without God and you have nothing at all!" God can't work on you with obstacles/obstructions in the way, remove the block and God will do a good work in you (Phil 2:13-16). Are you ready to forgive and get a vision? Are you willing to obey God and forgive (Isa. 1:19-20)? Leaders need to have a clean heart and the right spirit. Be on fire for the Lord, bringing fuel to the fire because your light has run out, you have no more fire burning and your fuel is very low. You have to have a burning desire for God, for a vision and adding fuel to the fire to keep you motivated. When you are on fire for God or a career, you don't have time for pity party, being disrespectful, talking ugly about the same things over and over when you know it upsets you.

Be aware of the temptation and the words you use. An awesome leader wants to help, lead and guide. Avoid following a male/female who talks about others behind their backs. Avoid people who speak evil, do evil and are jealous. We all need somebody who can build us up when we are down or have fallen so deep into the hole. But everything starts at home. We have to pray the will of God, daily (meaning the words in the Bible) and not wanting revenge. God doesn't hear evil prayer, only His words from the Bible. If you don't know how to pray, that is how, using God's word! Please have a clear understanding of what the Bible teaches because there are very few laborers who follow and do the will of God. Some never went out in the street and witnessed to people or win souls to God. That is why they don't know how to handle bad circumstances. Others are in the world suffering even more but you don't know because you never try to help anyone, but are very good at trying to hurt many. You need healing, you don't listen to your Pastor, people who try to help you and we won't take good advice from people who feel your pain! There are too many of us suffering out here. Become a leader, get active in helping others, show love and get an idea of doing something great for God.

# Without My Father

In the world today, there's plenty of children who grew up without a father. And their father who grew up without a father, also. Fathers do play a big role in children lives. Boys and girls are really suffering without their dads. They feel left without answers. Which children hurt the most: male/female? Who knows! It affects each child differently. Some dads don't know how to love, talk and have a nice time with their kids because his own father never did anything with him. That's why you hurt and your dad is hurting also because his father never showed him real love. Having both parents in your life and able to talk with both parents is very important. The reason your father never talked, spent time with you and showed no love; maybe he has a lot of guilt and pain built up inside of him from his dad. Children depend on both parents, for love, trust, and protecting. Parents are the ones who speak kind words, encourage their child, build them up when they are at their lowest point and watch after them. Children want to feel that love, joy, peace, feel the support, happiness and want to know that they are valuable to their parents. When the parents separate, the children always suffer and feel depressed. They feel let down by their dad/mom, disappointed, depressed, abandoned, sad, angry, lost and helpless. Men and women, you want to stay in contact with your children; no matter what happens in your marriage or relationships. There are thousands of relationships and marriages that fall apart but the kids are still here. You are not the only ones. Dad, your children still need to talk with you, spend time with you, express their feelings and show how much you love your children. If you had other children with someone else, still don't abandon your first children because they didn't ask to be here. Maybe your father abandoned you but you can change that family tree and love your kids. Let them be around their other siblings because some people end up dating and marrying their brother or sister because they didn't know or found out when it was too late.

Children experience fear and have a rough time without their dad or mother. Men/Women, don't put the absent parent down because you are sad with him/her, but tell the truth. Help your children to have a good relationship with their dad. I understand he hurt your feeling but life goes on, the beat goes on and the beat goes on and on. It can be hard sometimes, if the man doesn't have enough balls to speak up and let his mate know that he will see his children because they were there before he/she came into the picture. Especially if you never let anyone come between you and your kids and you always talk to them. Men, it's your job to call and say hello to your children. Some men avoid calling or won't continue to have a relationship because you have more children and think you now have to put out more money. Money can't buy love, it's about showing you care, spending some time together, a hug, a smile and a little conversation. There are plenty of things to do to show God's agape kind of love, without spending money. Don't let them continue to grow old and die without knowing, did my dad really love me, because he never showed it? You may be in a marriage or relationship but learn to communicate with your partner because without communication; you have no relationship at all. Men, speak up and do what God would have you to do. Did God disown you? Did God show you love and make you feel unwanted? Your children feel unwanted and need you to talk to them. It hurts to feel neglected by someone who helped created you to be born into his world. Without a father, it can block children's vision and many end up doing bad things and making bad choices. Some children, the mom raised them very nicely and the children are doing well. But it still doesn't give you as a dad an excuse to not have a better relationship with your children.

Ms. Star is a young lady in her late 20s now. Her dad left when she was about two years old. She remembers her dad used to pick her and her brother up sometimes. Years later she didn't see him at all, for a while. At age seven, Star remembers her dad coming to her mom's home and letting them know he was going to get married. The children were in the wedding and about a year later, the relationship ended. When Star was 15 going on 16, she was feeling a tremendous anger against her dad. She wanted to tell her mom but didn't know how. Star was so upset with her dad and wondered what happened to their relationship. It caused her bad headaches and depression inside of her. Star ended up in the hospital for a week. Her mother still didn't know why Star was depressed. Months went by and Star wrote a letter to her mom and one for her dad. She wrote her mom a letter saying, I appreciate you for so many things. One thing I appreciate you for is being here for me at all times (unlike my father). I appreciate you for still buying me Christmas stuff even though we aren't doing so good financially. I thank you for giving me money when I needed it and giving me insight about life and boys. I appreciate you being a strong woman because our family has been through so much. But you continue to stand strong. I appreciate you for being my role model and you taught me so many things every day and probably don't even notice it. You have taken me places and I thank you. One day, I will get my own car and take some stress off of you. One more thing I want to say is I appreciate you for doing your best for me. Love you, your one and only daughter. I can't say that about Daddy, he's got other kids and where did his love go for me? She wrote this letter 1/23/2006. Star has been thinking about her father for years, maybe when holidays came around, her birthday, day to day, months and years about their relationship without her dad.

Star wrote a letter also to her dad on May 25, 2006. Without my father! I sit here and wonder does he love me. He says it but does he really mean it, because he sure doesn't show it. He doesn't see the pain he's causing me. It seems that this hole in my heart is getting bigger and bigger and bigger. All the betrayal, all the pain. I just can't take this anymore. I feel let down by the man that meant the most to me in my life. I sit here and wonder, what do I mean to him. Am I just a child that doesn't matter anymore since I'm near grown? I need just as much attention as any other child. I sit here and wonder, do I deserve to be treated like this, to be last on his list. Does he not know that I have needs and he is a big part of it? I find myself thinking about this often and sometimes I cry myself to sleep just thinking about it. Am I a child he doesn't want to claim anymore? If so, why didn't he tell me this before. I sit here and wonder why does he give me money. I mean, it is always a plus but does he feel sorry for me. Money doesn't heal a relationship. If he can give me money, why can't he show me love? I sit here and wonder how often does he think about me. I sit here and think about what happened to our relationship. I sit here and think about what could've been, shouldn't been. Wouldn't have been and what will never be. But the one thing Star think about most is does he love her. Some children take a long time to heal when abandoned by a parent. It's not too late to make amends with one another.

Fathers, avoid leaving your children rejected, with a heavy heart, a heartache, feeling lonely, hurt and without answers. While you are still alive fill that gap and build that bridge of love. The kids feel unloved and unwanted. It costs you nothing but a little time, kind words, a hug and some of your love from the heart. Build something special between you and your children, something that will last a lifetime. A bond that no one can come in between or break. A good relationship with your child brings joy and happiness. Star still feels the grief, sadness and suffers the loss of her dad's relationship, emotionally throughout her life. Divorce, remarriage, and separation leave a child devastated and disowned. Seek to connect with your child because you don't want to leave this earth without saying good-bye and how you feel about each other. There are dads who hide their depression, they fear to connect with their children because of the new woman in their lives or new family. Many are afraid to face their fears of losing the new relationship or new marriage instead of talking about it. Many fathers cry in the dark and live silence for years. Just like the children, cry, keep silent, let their anger build up inside, they grow demons and giant monsters which will be ready to act out. Quiet anger is dangerous. Confront your fear with your partner, your new kids and connect back with your first children.

Stop living in your past hurts, confront that one bad apple in your life and love all your kids.

Express how you are feeling from the heart. Tell the truth and stop letting these toxic marriage and relationship take you away from your children. Life isn't fair and we can't really depend on earthly people to give and show us love. Sad to say, that includes your parents as well. Many of us are church goers but still don't love some of our children, like we should. We all are adults and know right from wrong. Are you feeling a lot of guilt? Get it right with God, forgive yourself and ask your children to forgive you too. Men, do you have any idea what ship never sinks? A friendship with you and all your children. Meaning your friendship. Your children that are stressed, and need some energy. You are the one that can bring that friendship back and bring fuel to their dryness on the inside. Their fire is very low, from being unwanted and unloved. They want you to provide lots of fuel to their fire, to sparkle it up. They want it to burn normal again. You all can start the recovery stage and grow a better relationship. There's always more room for self-improvement, to do better, personal growth, self-support, and self-love. We all just want to be loved. How would you feel if your dad treated you this way? Maybe your dad did, but you don't have to treat your kids that way. Pick up the pieces to the puzzle and find what's missing. A good face to face talk will solve some or all of the pain. Children's hearts are damaged, sinking and need help to swim. Step up and be the dad you once were or start from where you are to build a relationship. If you don't know how, go to your Lord and Savior Jesus Christ. Time is running out and life is very short. The Coronavirus disease has no name on it, let's love one another while we can. They are just a phone call away. AMEN.

# Let Go of Hatred, Forgive and Get a Vision

Many people are filled with regret, they are concerned about what to do because a husband, wife, friends or parent have walked out of their life or someone dear to them has passed away. They are afraid to love again, hurting, refuse to get help, need to be healed but are putting it off and refuse to be healed. They are so wounded; they try to be tough; strong; they repeat themselves daily by speaking evil and are really weak. A strong-minded person doesn't keep repeating themselves, only hurting people that are in pain. They say the same thing over, over and over again. They talk about old stuff for days, weeks, months and years, just repeating themselves over and over again. It is sad to hold on to things that drag a person down for a lifetime. A tough strong man/woman leaves the past behind. They get stronger from their past experiences and get away from being angry. You hate someone so much it's not that serious, it's not a joke because you want to get even. But you are mad because people don't care how mad you are because it is pointless, being angry and blaming others. You have no clue that their mind is focused on God and not on you. They are traveling, doing great things and enjoying their lives. You upset, crying, angry, hopeless, jealous, and holding hatred inside of you. Jesus loves us all and He is a forgiving God. Are you getting pleasure out of revenge on another? Well, God doesn't approve of your wrong desire and wrong behavior! What are you afraid of, other than once disappointed? Live your life. They have moved on, achieving their goal, dream and a vision? That is because they are thinking positive and not evil things. You have the opportunity to do the same things, once you get over the past and bitterness in your life. You are digging yourself in a deeper in a hole, full of roadblocks.

Is there anything that you would want to do that is positive? Where is your motivation, desire and plan for the future? Being afraid and fearing pain, it is keeping you from a joyful life. Living in the past is destroying you and will carry hatred to your kids. Mature, grow up, and ask God to clean you up and create in you a new spirit. Get yourself a new heart and a new spirit (Ezekiel 18:31). Renew your mind and remove the mask. (Romans 12:2) we have to be transformed by the renewing of your mind. Be a living sacrifice to our Lord and Savior Jesus Christ. Others see your pain because of the way you talk, act, and the stream of smoke coming from you. It is like you are about to blow up the world because of one or two people you think caused you pain. Let not your heart be troubled, (John 14:1) because God the way, the truth, the light and the life. AMEN. Have you ever made a mistake? Are you listening to God and not your stormy hard heart? You need a new heart and God wants to operate on you, so you can forgive and feel better. Do you like torturing others you are blaming? Does that make you feel like you are in control, even though they are not stooping to your level? We all need to give/show kindness because love covers a multitude of sins (Proverbs 10:12). Hatred stirs up strife, but love cover all sins. Have a great lifestyle, you want people to follow the love inside of you and for others, it is so important to love and forgive. If you are still holding grudges you are not fully mature and are still developing. Many see the way you live (your lifestyle), by your attitude. Your angry emotion shows you are weak and not strong. The past has full control over the mind and body. You need to shake off those horrible past feelings. Wake Up, Wake Up! God needs you in His army to help hurting people, and if you are hurting you can't help anyone because you are all on the same ship. You are on the path of destruction and destroying many lives. Turning them away from the Savior. There are others that are seeking payback too, but they will also hurt until they forgive. Stop making more pain for yourself and others.

Are you being ignorant to the Bible and have hidden bruises inside of you? Do you not know the consequence for your reactions? A strong dislike, strong hatred, hidden secrets and you think no one sees it! What a tragedy to carry around unhealed wounds for the rest of your life? Do not lead us into temptation but deliver us from evil (Matthew 6:13). Where is the power for the future, because the past destroys all the future plans? When you talk about hurting, it fires you up, push the bomb button, and you are irritated again. (James 3:6) don't have a tongue on fire that defiles the whole body. Be on fire for God, bring fuel to the fire because His word is like fire shut up in your bones. When you love God, and are on fire for Him and a burning desire, there is no way you can keep it to yourself. He has been so good to you, better than you've been to yourself. There is a way that seems right to a man but the end leads to death (Proverbs 16:25). Your tongue should heal one another and not ruin lives or bring them to your level of hatred (Proverb 12:18). Watch the words you say that come out of the mouth, meaning be slow to speak and think. What's your burning desire? Is it to create and bring danger into existence, to commit evil acts and wanting to hurt that person really bad for the past homesickness? If so, that is not the right way; let go, let God in and start getting a vision. Stop being afraid of past regrets and get concerned with forgiving a loved one, so you can be set free.

Share your frustration and pain with the men/women in the past that you are blaming. Are you ashamed and want to keep your pride of anger going on? Do you see the pain isn't going anywhere? Come out of the darkness and remove hatred from the mind. Don't be afraid to forgive a loved one and many others. Your pride will keep you pointless, clueless, envious, frustrated, in grief, loneliness and you have no clue that you are causing harm to yourself and bring sickness to the body. Get out of the darkness and come into the light. Stop leaning into your own understanding, especially if it is evil work because it is unhealthy for the mind. Many fail because of doubt, excuses, blame game, fear, anger, past, rejection to do right, and ignoring the problem. We must talk the pain out, get to the bottom/root of what is truly stressing a person out. Do you feel 100% confidence that the act of wrongdoing is what will make you feel better? And do you feel it is working? Are your results still the same and do you feel much better? Are you feeling worse?

Stop running from your past and go to the people you are blaming and communicate. Talk about what's causing you fear and having a trouble harden heart. If you keep hiding, holding serious pain inside, and not facing a person, one on one or face to face, the upsets will never leave the brain. It becomes a dangerous mind. A mind that don't care, and abuse the spiritual walk with Jesus Christ. You have stopped pressing toward the high calling, which is in Jesus and forgot what He has called you to do (Philippians 3:14). Many never found their purpose on earth or their place in God. When we turn to darkness, leave the Kingdom of light after going to church for so many years, it shows the counterfeit in a child of the Most High God. You need to be grounded in God's Word, that is where your help comes from. Not from other hurting people, depressed or stressed out people. Keep on living, you will need God again. There is too much happening in the world today and you might need that person who you are blaming all your problems on. Everyone is unique in their own way, refuse to let one thing stop you from a goal or vision. The dreams and visions are something we should be looking forward to in this life. Make peace, face your fear head on, and forgive, or are you ashamed to speak peace? Don't keep allowing Satan to steal your joy and turn you into something you never were. There are plenty who were never obeying or walking righteously in the Lord because Satan goes to the house of God daily too. Just hope you weren't the one who had one foot in the Kingdom and one foot in the world. It does show, and people are looking at you. You give yourself away by your reaction, especially walking away from Christ and plotting to harm others. Get a vision, get yourself together, start loving each other, you are perishing away because you don't obey God. Love has a lot to do with your living here on earth. Remember that song, "What's love got to do with it?" It plays a big part in healing the mind and body. We need a healing, mind renewed, body transformed and we need it right away, not later. NOW. Your faith is being tested.

# Is Church Stopping You?

◇◇◇◇◇◇◇◇◇◇◇◇◇◇◇◇◇◇◇◇◇◇◇◇◇

Are you having trouble in church? Is it the church or is it you? Take a look at yourself. How do you see yourself and what is your future life looking like? There are many women/men that complain about church hurt. Can you see what is really going on inside of you? You may need the Lord to search you from head to toe. If you attend church services or have been going for years: has anything changed in your life? Are you still the same because something should have changed, even if it is something small? Find a strong church, people who are on fire for the Lord and are truly committed to Him. An organized church, that holds services on time and meet your needs as well as other people. Jesus Christ is our best friend we can ever have in this world. When you commit yourself fully to Him, you will start seeing Christ moving in and through you. Most males/females don't read the Bible, don't have an intimate relationship with Christ, and never pray on their knees. Maybe your faith is what's got a stronghold on you and the music you listen to also can divide churches. Looking at the thing boys/girls are doing in this world doesn't mean you should do it. We all know what is good and what is bad, what we should do and should not do. You just should live by faith, so your faith will determine how you live, your attitude toward many, how many people you lead to Christ, your love toward others, who you are following, your leadership, are you taking notes in church, and are you building people up or pulling them down.

If you don't have joy in your heart, it can stop you from moving forward because you might be plotting to harm someone.

Without being filled with the Holy Spirit, can deathly keep you in your old sin nature and hold you back from what God has for you. When you neglect the fellowship focus on God in church service and your mind is on looking for a woman/man or going to church for all the wrong reason. Some go to talk about people and you are no better and have no more than what they have. Most males/females are living paycheck to paycheck, so no one is better and God loves all of us the same. Many of us do want to do better financially, make more money, live peacefully, have nice things and better ourselves. That is why we have the Bible, the Holy Spirit and God the Father, to help us while here on this earth. The Lord will show us where to go, where not to go and tell us the truth. His Bible is our handbook and He want us to use it daily. If people follow you, will your church be stronger or are you help making your church be weaker because of your bad behavior? Ask God to search your heart and renew the right spirit in you. Many don't believe the word of God, they just go to gossip, see what they see, and think they are doing God a favor, to say they go to church or to dress up. But God is not impressed! He wants us all to be filled with the Holy Spirit, have Spirit filled leadership in the church, meet the needs of many, and show His agape kind of love and not that evil attitude.

You can't do His work without being filled with the Holy Spirit because the Holy Spirit will convict you when you are doing something wrong and if it's not pleasing to the Lord. And that is missing in so many people's lives; that might be why we can't forgive, are still sinning, still sleeping around, still lying, keep committing adultery, won't let go of that stinky attitude, and don't know how to love people because you don't love yourself. How can you love anyone, if you've got a bad attitude and don't even love yourself? Check yourself and have a nice long talk with your Savior, He is the only one who can help you. We should be reaching people with God's agape love. You have been going through this stronghold for too long now, around in a circle, a merry go round and you can't stop it. You need help from above, God has that power to help you. Get committed and filled with the Holy Spirit now, that might be why you are struck. You are leading people away from the Lord and making your Pastor look bad because of your sinful ways and the words that come out of your mouth, you defile a man. We are the body of Christ and He wants us all to live an abundant life. Has someone told you it is ok to drink, that is a weak church, founded on a strong church. That is a conviction and compromise against the word of God. There are many parents who attend church but have abandoned their children for no reason. Are you reading your Bible and what have you learned? How do you feel when the Pastor preaches a sermon about children are a gift from God? The Holy Spirit is there to bring all things to our remembrance. Get a vision, do something with your life besides staying bitter.

# Are Your Finances A Problem?

◇◇◇◇◇◇◇◇◇◇◇◇◇◇◇◇◇◇◇◇◇◇◇◇

Many ladies/guys don't know what they want to do and don't know how to make big bucks. Try a business that you know is good for everyone and has products that everyone can use or need. We pay all this money going to college, to get licenses and there are businesses out here where you pay little to nothing for a license, to start a business. You have to have a willing mind, lots of energy, on fire, a ready mind, be excited, a listening mind and open mind, if you want to make big money. It doesn't hurt to try something new and if the person is telling you the truth and being honest, why not try it? And you won't have to go to a job but it will be your own business. We need a goal in place, for our future retirement. Pray to God about everything and walk in the Holy Spirit. Everyone needs God in their life. Learn to have an intimate relationship with Jesus, so He can work in our life. If you are walking in the flesh, it is not the spirit of God. It is a time and season for everything. Start thinking, searching, praying about a vision. You will need a backup plan. Many people are time broke and money broke.

It would be nice to have a business, with no limits on how much money you can earn. Very few people have a dream life. Many will work for the rest of their lives. They will either have all the money they need to take care of themselves for the rest of their life, or work until it's time to leave this earth. Because that is what we all were taught, to work and never talk about family business. Do you know why a marriage or relationship might fail? It's not always the sex, but not enough money. We all need to do better in this area in our life. You are not alone. Focus on something you and your spouse would like to have in the future. Do you have the money, or how long would it take to get the money? It's time to start planning and find ways to grow your finances. Get the big picture in your mind and go for it. Take your income and build something great for you and your family. You don't want to stay in one spot. You have been going around in that circle for too long. Move and don't look back, get help if you need it and push yourself to succeed. Success is not an accident but a blessing from God.

When having a business or learning to save money, you'll need to have self-discipline, self-improvement, and self-help. No more excuses, instead use you mind to do something great. Gain momentum and take action. Don't let your pride keep you in bondage, do something awesome. Have you ever through about having money working for you while you are sleep? Having money just rolling into your account. Most of the time we are in our own way and most of the time someone is in our ear, telling us what we can and can't do. There are males/females who make excuses, don't care to have better things, don't think they can change, don't want to change, don't know how to change, feel they can never have great things or lots of money. Many stay stuck and never change. They always complain about not having money, they cry broke and want a handout. Do you know the difference between the people who have money and the people with no money? The people with money know where to put their money so it can grow, compound interest. They have a financial coach, who shows them how to grow millions of dollars. It's better to start saving while you are young and don't tell anyone how much you saved, unless you and your mate are working together on a vision. If you tell others they will want some for free, when they can do what you are doing, saving. Please teach your children to save early in life. We seem to put our own self down. We don't believe we can have great things or big money. Our parents didn't have and we think it's impossible for us to have.

Let's think about all the years we all worked. Do you have any idea where your money went? Did you save any of the money? How many years have you worked and how much did you make? Many make six figures and still have nothing saved. The more you make, the more you spend. It's important to know where your money is going and a have a plan to save. Males/Females will work a job but are not willing to become wealthy for themselves or their children. We need to get educated on finances because knowledge is power. Without the proper finance, we are lost, and the mind can't think. Get rid of all the garbage in your mind, all the dead relationships, and find new friends. Clean it all out and get a fuel injection, to help get the mind moving and flowing in the right direction. We are off track and need the mind to think fast because some of us are getting older. It's too late to change the past, we have to start where we are at now. How many of us have been nailed down, lazy, always tired, using the kids as an excuse, scared of success and not holding yourself accountable? Maybe you are scared of success because you know you would have to put in some work in and you don't want that commitment. Guess what else you won't have? That money that we all need, to take care of us for the rest of our life. Many are grown and still live with their parents, never worked, don't want to work or do a business but are always asking others for money. Get a job, if you don't want a business of your own and stop running behind these men that mean you no good. Do something great for you and your children. Many do anything for these men but not for yourself and your children.

If you want something great, appreciate what God has already done for you. If you want to do better, you must have a burning desire, work hard, work smart, attack blessing, make no excuses, make adjustments in your life, face your fears, change the things that pull you down and cause you pain. Your energy has to be right and ready to go. Have a character development for a vision, building something unique. Stop thinking negative before you even start something great. Negative thinking can hold a person back from some great opportunities. Stop thinking you can't handle success and try it. Change is wonderful, there is growth in changing and helping you to eliminate all distractions. Avoid letting anyone destroy your vision. Make sure all your finances are lined up and in order. The right amount of life insurance, and the right kind, can save you from a headache. Always read your policy, just don't go and sign something. Read the small words, the fine print, so you won't be disappointed later on in life. Let's brainstorm, take your age and see how much money you would need to save every week, bi-weekly or monthly to have a million dollars or more to retire on, or money that will last for the rest of your life. Do you see why our children need to save now? Example: A person who is 25-65 would need to save about $158 a month at 1% will they have a million! Banks don't give you enough interest for your money to grow, meaning you will need a coach. It matters where they put their money at 3%, 5%, 10%, 12% makes a big difference in how much money they would have. You need to know the rule of 72, your fin number and know where to put your money. Get a coach to help you out with investing and saving. Please get educated on money, life insurance, investing, banks, saving, stock and bonds. You want to be prepared when disaster or storms come. The

Coronavirus caught everyone off guard and many with no financial plan, no savings and no emergency money. It's a blessing to have money put away and plenty of money at retirement. Retirement is not about the age; it's about how much money you accumulate so you can stop working when you feel like it.

# Emotions, Are They Holding You Back?

◇◇◇◇◇◇◇◇◇◇◇◇◇◇◇◇◇◇◇◇◇◇◇◇

There are plenty of emotions, feelings, thinking wrong and insecurity. Learn to pray the model prayer when problems come. (Matthew 6-5:13) "and do not lead us into temptation but deliver us from evil ones." A mind is a terrible thing to throw away. Everything starts with our mind and the way we think about different situations. Maybe you have caused harm to a friend, neighbor, co-worker or family member. You could have talked negatively about many males/females because you didn't have much growing up. Your emotions change because only one parent raised you. Some blessings and goals are not met because you are blocking them by being disrespectful to a parent and others. (Romans 1:30-32) backbiters, haters of God, violent, proud, boasters, inventors of evil things, disobedient to parents, undiscerning, untrustworthy, unloving, unforgiving, unmerciful; who, knowing the righteous judgment of God, that those who practice such things are deserving of death. Be careful when practicing hatred. Many think bad things because they have plenty of time on hand. They have no job, stayed at home with children, refuse to work, marriage/relationship ended badly, lazy, don't want to do anything but gossip, hate a person because they look better than you and don't like people because they are doing great things for themselves and their family. Many just have too much time on their hands because they have nothing to do but think too much. But they think of all the wrong stuff, meaning negative things because they are disappointed. They always forget the things that they did and said about others out of their mouth. (Matthew 15:11,18) Not what goes into the mouth defiles a man; but what comes out of the mouth, this defiles a man. (Matthew 18) But those things which proceed out of the mouth comes from the heart and they defile a man. And how they were forgiven by many girls/boys including our Lord and Savior Jesus Christ.

With bad emotions ruining/running your life, you will not make it too far in life. (Acts 17:30) Truly, these times of ignorance God overlooked, but now "commands all men everywhere to repent." Be interested in a goal and have people following you. Avoid being bored, zoned out (apathy) for years and plotting to hurt human beings. For the wages of sin is death, but with God the gift is eternal life in Christ Jesus our Lord. (Romans 6:23). Wrong behavior and wrong thinking can have a human put away for a lifetime and they will lose their mind. Are you on drugs and don't know what have been going on from day to day, week to week, month to month and year to year? Well, you don't have to keep living like that because Jesus Christ has paid for all of our sins. You just have to make your mind up and turn to Jesus Christ for help. He cares for you; He loves us all and your family loves you too. They just want to see you do better, let go of things which are keeping you down and destroying the mind. Do you see how bad habits are a disaster to the body and mind, how it's killing you? You have no room to think positive and have no idea of the bad things you are doing. It is holding you back from spending time with family, caring for the kids properly, you forgot about your career/dreams and many are preforming and doing messes they never dreamed about doing. You got caught up in that moment and can't shake that demon off of you. (Acts 17-28) "for in Him we live and move." You have to get out of that mess and bad thinking habit. We all need to love each other, pray for the world, pray for equal justice and peace and pray about the deaths from the Virus. By giving love, showing love and doing what the Bible commands, we can change this world to be a better place. Stop the violence and change your emotions.

Is your body weakened, worried, wicked, gotten wild, using it as a weapon to harm, and is it weighed down? You shouldn't be feeling like this, especially if you are living for the Savior. (1 Corinthians 2:10) To overcome this weakness, everyone will need spiritual wisdom. "But God has revealed them to us through His Spirit, For the Spirit searches all things, yes, the deep things of God." The ones that don't know Him, read your Bible, all should read your Bible to get a good understanding. We are missing something awesome in our lives and need to "meditate on the Word of God daily." (Proverbs 11:5) The righteousness of the blameless will direct his way aright. But the wicked will fall by his own wickedness." You have let small circumstances bring you down to your knees and can't get back up. The only reason you should be down on your knees; is praying to God because of your weakness. On your knees giving Glory only in the Lord. But the devil is living in and through you and you don't realize it. (1 Corinthians 1:27) But God has chosen the foolish things of the world to put to shame the wise, and God has chosen the weak things of the world to put to shame the things which are mighty. Stop letting the devil of this world run your life. We have control over the devil, but we keep letting him into our life. The Lord give power to the weak and we must use it. (Isaiah 40:29, 31) He gives power to the weak; And to those who have no might, He increases strength. He will give you strength, those who wait on the Lord, shall renew their strength." The wicked shall be turned into hell, and all the nations that forgot God (Psalm 9:17). Many have let their pride stop them from forgiving others. It is time to wake up, you are adults now and acting like when you were a child and some are acting like their shoe size.

Mike had become so weak over the last 12 years. His marriage was broken and he didn't know how to fix it. The couple never went to church and he never accepted Jesus Christ as his Lord and Savior. He always ran his mouth as though he knew everything. He never wanted to listen to positive business men/women and just knew he had it going on. Most people are intimidated by people who make more money than them. Or people who are really trying to better their lives. One day the couple met Ms. Thacker, a woman who loves helping people.

Ms. Thacker expresses the importance of how to have passive income, retirement income and she talk to the couple about their fin number. Mike tuned it out and thought he had it going on because he had some money saved but don't know anything about a fin number. Lots of ladies/men are just struck in their old ways which is working for others for the rest of their lives. They cry about being broke, wish they didn't have to get up, always late for work, don't like the job they do, get paid and pay bills, have no money to enjoy, live paycheck to paycheck and are just miserable. But they refuse to try out new opportunities, that women/men offer. Many people don't want anything and won't help a family member, friend or neighbor out with their business. They never spread the word around and put the loved one's name out there to help support their business. Many don't want you to get ahead of them or they don't want to see you succeed with anything. These are the ones who say they love you but won't support you. These people stay broke for the rest of their lives because of a lack of knowledge. Try some of the meetings and workshops others offer, if you know you don't have any money saved; what do you have to lose? Nothing; so why not try it! God brings people into your life for all kinds of reasons. And this might just be your season to try bigger and better things. This might be the right time for you to make big money and get a business rolling.

There was a group of women, who were all raised by their dad. They never liked any of the jobs they worked at and would always quit and find another job. They tried to go to college but never pursued what they went for. Terry was the aunt, she told the young ladies, let's talk to the family and talk about a business we can all do. But no one wanted to talk about that. Nowadays family still won't talk about a business because it is something most black people don't talk about. there might be some, but very few. People will not stick by each other or support one another, sad but true facts. It's been like this forever.

No one wants to change or leave their children or family an inheritance. We are used to not owning anything or having any kind of family companies. Many just work hard and not smart. Some are weak minded and can't think for themselves. Terry explained to her nieces, how her mother and father passed away but had no money to leave her. Terry had to collect money to bury her parents because they had no investments, no savings and no life insurance. She told her niece if her parents would have had enough life insurance, a good amount of coverage, she could have buried them, paid the house off and the car. But many today feel they don't need life insurance, a savings or investment and some have no clue that they need to have all these things in place. When the struggles come, the pain comes, the depression comes and next you are carrying around a heavy weight. Your burdens are just too oppressively heavy.

# Ingredients Help with a Vision

◇◇◇◇◇◇◇◇◇◇◇◇◇◇◇◇◇◇◇◇◇◇◇◇◇

The right ingredients can make all the difference in a person's life. What kind of ingredients are you feeding the mind and soul? Jesus Christ should be your first ingredient. Make sure you have a strong desire for what you do. It should benefit many people and it should be helpful. Good ingredients can set you free from the past and bad ingredients can ruin your life forever. Bad decisions can ruin the most important things that are close to you and can take away your strength to heal the mind. To lose what you love, has caused you to ruin yourself. Being worried over the past will weaken the mind and make you spread rumors about people you love. How does a rumor get started? It is started by jealous people, so-called friends, how many of us have them? Friends, the ones we can depend on, friends, how many of us have them? Friends is a word we use every day but most of the time we use it in the wrong way! You can look the word up but many of us don't know the meaning of friends. We have a friend Who sticks closer than a brother, family or friends, and His name is Jesus. He is the number #1, He is food on the soul, good ingredients, and will be there forever. He is a friend to the end. When you die to the past, God is able to take you higher to where He wants you to be. He doesn't want you to be disappointed for the rest of your life. He has plan for your life, so even when life has let you down, refuse to be bitter. You have a calling on your life, to help others. Don't let one bad potato ruin your happiness, get up and let God love you. You need God to love you and heal the heart. God will give you better ingredients to fix what is wrong but you have to remove the corrupt thinking patterns.

Just because people or loved ones have left your side, they don't want you to continue having a pity party. They would want to see to live your dream and get a vision. Not crying all the time, starting trouble but be a peacemaker with God's love. Stop being mad with God, or saying there is no God (Psalm 53:1-4). God does chastise His children whom He loves, and will correct us (Job 5:17). Avoid being wax cold, confused, a mind out of control, being violent, worried and becoming worthless. You should always be able to share the good news about Jesus Christ. Jesus is the same every day, He doesn't change like we do. One moment we are on fire for God, next we are lukewarm, dead church, faith ran out, we are corrupt, and are partaking in evil acts. Wanting to get even, letting temptation into the heart. Teaching your children what you were taught and showing them how you live life according to your feelings. Have faith, believe it, read it, obey the word, have favor with God, fear God only and not man. Then you will be able to have victory in your life and not pass curse down to the children. God loves you and so do other loved one, so why are you still wanting to hurt friends and family? You don't have to hurt, but it your choice whether or not to live in the past of corruption and complaining (Isaiah 41:10). God is with us, if you allow Him to enter into your heart.

Everything has its time (Ecclesiastes 3:1-8). A time for healing, peace, be transformed, time to die, to keep silence, time to dream, time to forgive, to let go of the past, time to build yourself up, speak, love, laugh, sing, dance, and make amends with and love people with whom you have been angry. Shake off the foolishness, flattering tongue, confusion gathering others into your bitterness and establish something better in your life instead of strife. Payback is something because karma will get you back. Don't think nothing can happen to you, you are the one plotting to commit evil acts and wrongdoing to others. Why allow one thing to change your attitude, make you walk in darkness and change your name?

Your evidence shows your weak spot, you are helpless and need God's grace and mercy now. We can do all that evil, but the only thing that matters while we are on this earth, is what we do for Jesus Christ will last and will be counted. So, don't let problems, situations, circumstances and the devil, change you because you can't fix the anger. Go to the person head on, pray and go to God. When you forgive it is for you to move in your destiny and it also can help lead the other person to Jesus Christ. Then you all can and will feel better. Stop lacking the Word of God, but obey, obey and obey it! The Bible is our guide, direction, protection, food to the soul, our helper, redeemer and light to our path. Bible—our basic instruction before leaving this earth. You are stuck because you haven't been fully made whole, never been filled with the Holy Spirit and disobey God's command! These things help with bad times and hardship, when we are rooted and grounded in the Word of God. Not doing what we feel because we are miserable! Miserable people love company and hurting people hurt people. Karma will step in when the right time comes. God gives all of us time to get it right, it's our decision to do right or continue to destroy because of jealousy and bitterness. You are not alone!

The main ingredient that you need, is to be sold out to God. Let Him just love you because we look for love in all the wrong places and end up getting our hearts hurt. We hunger, thirst, and put our trust in the wrong people and things. Clear your view because you can't serve two masters, serving God and Satan makes you become double-minded, not understanding that what you are doing is wrong. You need fruit in your life, which is love. Are you committing a conspiracy? Has someone left you for someone else, so you go get in a relationship knowing the pain your lover left you with, and you carry it into another relationship. You don't want that man/woman but you need to heal the pain, but the pain won't leave. That is because you are in a relationship for the wrong reason (to get even). Are you having children by people you don't love, or marry someone you don't love because you are doing what others are doing? You are hurting so bad that you don't know what to do, because with what you are doing the past pain is still there. You are only becoming more, more, and more unhappy. Still smiling around friends and family you love, hiding behind a mask and crying on the inside.

Wake Up, Wake Up! You are getting the same result from your past relationships. Take time out! How do you want your life to be, happy or sad, peaceful or worried, stay lost or get a vision, live in the dark or get some light? Let God love you and take care of you, many find that hard to do. But until you do, your life will keep going in circles because what you are looking for you can't see. There are signs and evidence of proof which is right in your face, but the eye is blind and the path is a dark and long journey ahead. Get the ingredients that you need, life is short and time will not go back and repeat itself.

# Vision—Taking Trips

◇◇◇◇◇◇◇◇◇◇◇◇◇◇◇◇◇◇◇◇◇◇◇◇◇

Won't it be nice to be able to take husband/wife trips and family trips? Having all the money you need to pay for your room/board, food, go shopping and be debt free. When you do not have to be counting your change to make ends meet. Have traveling money for gas, rental cars, movies, and restaurants. Wining and dining your spouse while enjoying yourself. It is a wonderful thing to have money saved at retirement time. Some people don't have one hundred dollars in the bank, many don't have $500 and plenty doesn't have $1,000 saved up. You must think about what you want for you and your family. It is important to save and be debt free. If you are in debt, start finding ways to get out of it. It can take years just paying back $2,000, so anything more than that you are really in trouble. It is good to have a credit card or two but try not to have any at all. The best way is to pay cash money. Having too many credit cards will keep you stressed out and broke. Due to the virus 2020, avoid making more debt. We know some people are not making the money they used to because some businesses are shut down. But do your best with what you have and stay debt free. We all would like to have money and avoid being miserable because of a lot of bills. It will have you pulling your hair out and worried, why me? But the cards are how we are able to pay for things we want, when we don't have the money. Always try to buy things you really need, even though credit cards can still keep you in a bind. Credit cards can cause hardship, struggle and disappointment in your life. Avoid over charging a credit card. They can save you sometimes and can also put a hole in your pocket. Get a coach to help you manage your money, they are good with helping you save and grow your money. Coaches teach you how to avoid credit cards and use your own money.

Having all the money you need until death, will make life much easier for you. You and a loved one can take trips together or if you are single, you can enjoy your life and meet new people. It will help you to be happy and at peace. Many males/females dream about having money, nice cars, a dream house and no stress. It feels good to be successful and able to have things of your own and buy what you like. Take care of the family; retire with a smile on your face and have that peace of mind. Thinking about where you can travel or go and have a great time with loved ones, children and mate. You don't have to worry about who can go and who can't go on the trip. Sometimes we can only let one or two children go on a trip and the next year someone else can go. But if the money, finances, business and the mind is thinking correctly then we are able to do bigger and better things. Dream big dreams, dream on purpose, know that you are blessed and highly favored. Have respect and support a family member who has a business or is trying to get one started. If you had a business, you would want family to help, stand by your side and cheer you on. It is a shame, but so many of us don't support our own family but will cheer others on. Your family should be doing something wonderful also and not always watching everyone else succeed. What about your family? Do you have money like that? Do you wish you could do something that will bless others? What do you think you can do to make life much better for you? Go the extra mile and do what you think is impossible. You want to always try to keep the money and business in the family. But you must teach your children, so they can teach their kids.

Many are afraid of failure and they fear success. Why be afraid to move forward or to better your life? It is the best thing you could ever do, move higher and higher into a goal. Life just doesn't seem fair sometimes, but it is our decision to take control of our desire and what we believe we can do. Never put can't into your vocabulary! Won't it be something if we didn't need money? But money is one thing we need in the world, besides God, life insurance, investments, and all deal with money. Our number one priority in the world is Jesus Christ. He will help us through trials, pain and a messed up, mind. Get a goal and a vision. You deserve better; be smart and make that first move to a life of fulfillment. Let no male/female interfere with you wanting more for yourself, but do the darn thing. Find a business that will help you with success; one great company is Primerica. Primerica is a company that is faithful, tells you the truth, will stick by you, you will always be able to contact your coach/trainer, they help you with retirement, savings, insurance, will and many other finances. People think too small and never move from where they are at. "Dream big, go after what's yours, never give up, and keep moving. Refuse to look back until you reach the top." Thank God while you are making your moves, worship Him, praise God and dance your pain away. Help a loved one out; send people their way if you are not interested in their business. We should be happy for a child that has his/her own business. If they are trying to help people; help them out! Are they hurting people or building them up with knowledge? Why are you not supporting them? Follow a good leader who wants to see you do better. They want to show you that you can go places where you thought it was impossible or too big of a dream for you. Wouldn't you like to take those trips with cash money and not credit cards or no money? With a positive mindset you can make it. Start that vision now, for your career of success.

# VISION—FEARING GOD

◇◇◇◇◇◇◇◇◇◇◇◇◇◇◇◇◇◇◇◇◇◇◇◇◇◇

We all should thank God for heaven and earth, also thank Him for our parents. (Deuteronomy 6:2), "that you may fear the Lord your God, to keep all His statutes and His commandments which I command you." Because if it had not been for His son Jesus Christ, dying on the cross for us we might not be here or if it wasn't for our parents. So, our Lord and Savior gets all the praise and glory, Amen. When pursuing a vision, be a good follower, you always want to give back by showing respect, kindness and a good reputation. Leaving an impression on other people's lives, show them that happy heart and share God's love with the world. Leading people in the right direction, by being an awesome leader. Telling the world about Jesus Christ and what He has done for you. (Psalm 19;9). The fear of the Lord is clean, enduring forever: The judgements of the Lord are true and righteous altogether. Have people following your footsteps and spreading your name around the world. You need a drive to stay alive; a drive to take you to unknown places. A gas pedal to move forward, take off the mask and do the task, cast out the non-supporters; ask God how to give back to those who help you. Never give up what you start, try to help many persons out of the darkness, even though many refuses to move. Everyone can't go with you anyway because God has something only for you. They don't have to stay in last place forever but they have to make their own decision. (Proverbs 3:5-7) You want to trust in the Lord, lean not unto your own understanding. Acknowledge Him in all your ways and He will direct your path. Do not be wise in your own eyes; Fear the Lord and depart from evil. Get a vision based upon your desire, not your current circumstances. Have that burning desire to be on fire for that plan or purpose. Bringing fuel to the fire to let your light shine bright. You want the fire burning deep down inside your soul, so you can keep moving and getting more ideas. Why do you want to do it? Maybe to have more money, get a better home and vehicle, change your life, have a new attitude, get away from a job, explore your blessing, have something you can call your own and with your name on it. Maybe to travel the world, go shopping without a credit card, have no payment but use cash, and stay debt free.

Have a plan and sticking to it. Push all that junk and abuse to the side. Letting go of everything that had you blind and dumb. Get a vision to have an urgency to do what is necessary at the time. Being patient, waiting for the result to come which can take some time. Stay encouraged while being patient because help is on the way. There is a way out of no way, we just have to hold on a little while longer. God will make a way won't he, do it? Always do your best until a change come! Keep on moving! (Proverbs 17:22) A merry heart does good, like medicine. But a broken spirit dries the bones. It would feel good be able to help your mom and dad. They might need a new car, a house or bill paid off or you can help them get out of debt. Giving is a blessing, showing you care and appreciate everything you have. Appreciate God, parents, children, family, Pastor, church, neighbors and others in the world. There is so much to be thankful for, food on the table, roof over your head, all of your body parts, eyes to see, a nose to smell and you wake up this morning. God is a good. He is a great God, He's a good God and He can do anything, if we ask in His name. We need to count our blessings every day; all of our good days outweigh the bad days, Amen. Avoid complaining, stop making excuses, get rid of the guilt, stop blaming yourself and appreciate your life. God's been keeping you!" (Luke 22:32) "But I have prayed for you that your faith should not fail; and when you have returned to Me strengthen your brethren." What God has for you, it is for you. He will bring you out, if you allow

Him. Stop trying to hurt boys/girls by bringing up their old past. Every day is a day of thanksgiving, God's been so good to us, every day He's blessing us.

Men/Women, some are mad with their parents or loved ones. Whoever you are holding grudges against, let it go because that unexpected person will one day cross your path. Get a vision, forgive males/females and the pain/weight will be much easier on your body. It is too heavy to carry around. Drop all that baggage, dream big, make plans, write the goals down and do something nice for your parents and others. We are running out of time. You wouldn't be here if it wasn't for two people who brought you into this world. No matter what happens in your life, show love and let go of all the hatred. Is it really worth the heartache and bad memories? Being born is a gift from the Lord, born to be great, and showing love. Be glad because His grace and mercy has kept you alive. Come out of the dark grave, break the strongholds in your life, knockdown those gates, you are frozen, overcome fear and get rid of unforgiving spirits in the mind. Stop complaining, get over it, fill that empty spot with joy, laughter, and happiness by loving many. Break every chain, break every chain because there is power in the name of Jesus! When you forgive, be gentle, meek, show you care and give back to your parents, etc. Your body will start doing a new thing, start making amends with people who hurt/caused you pain and watch the mood change. The body will feel different, the mind will think good things and the attitude will begin to change. We fall down but we get up! We fall down but we get up! We are all God's children and He loves us all. It seems hard but you can do it, if you want a peace of mind. You can do it if you try.

# What is Your Vision?

Are you hoping for something great to happen in your life? There is so much going on in the year 2020. We have the killing by police, people disrespecting cops, tornados, wildfires, black lives matter and hurricanes, etc. Don't allow these things to hinder your dreams. We all need to pray and learn to get along. It's time for everyone to seek Jesus Christ because we all need Him now. Where is the love for one another? Well, don't wait for the one you call your other half to change because you can't change them. Only God can lead them on the right path to success. In the world today, the road seems dark/black and nowhere to go. But there is a road which leads to the light of glory and peace. Apart from God we are nothing and can do nothing. Go to God in prayer and ask about a vision for yourself and once you get it, go for it! Never look back unless it helps with a testimony and you now have victory over your past. Other than that, keep it moving and never look back. Wisdom should come out of your mouth, by using kind words. Avoid settling for less, letting a person use you and treating you like a nobody. Ask God to create in you a clean heart and renew a steadfast spirit with in you, (Psalm 51:10). Give Christ all your problems and reaffirm your love to Him. We know when things are not right in our life, we know what we want but don't always do what's right. Love never harms, hurts or shows hatred. Jesus Christ is the same yesterday, today and forevermore. Get a vision. If you have a person who is disrespectful, leave them, if they come back to you, he/she was yours, but if they don't, they never were yours. Time to start the journey, you have been on that black, dark road far too long. Wake up, wake up follow the road until you see the bright yellow, orange, red light, the rainbow in the sky. There will be a difference in the way you walk, talk, sing, and dance. A Vision, see the Light.

Having a state of mind to see, help you see things in a different way. You will be able to see people differently, instead of the wrong they've done. You would see the best in them like God sees in them. People with a strong vision focus on a purpose that exists, working smart, having a kind heart, a humble heart, a calm, gentle spirit while being patient with everyone. Having a strong passion or motion for the talent/ dream. When difficult circumstances arise, still persevere and continue to do the business or goal. Keep going when it seems like nothing is happening right away; it takes time. Be determined, follow your heart and be persistent. Instead of giving up, have a mind set on winning and gaining. Gather a team of serious people who want to succeed in life. Laugh together, work as one, sing together, pray, cheer each other on, always win souls to Christ and win as a team. We have a mission ahead of us and it is to retire early, enjoy life, be happy, and become all that you can. Always have confidence in a dream, vision and in yourself. Make no excuses for changing your life around, just go for it. Look beyond your faults and who let you down. Move to the next plan, always have a plan for yourself. Remember, God loves you, He has a purpose and a plan for our lives. Wake up, wake up and dream, dream big dream and get a VISION.

It is a shame because you can talk positive, give good advice, try to help others, show them the way, write it out for them on paper and still they will not take in the knowledge. I am talking about the ones murdering their people, people in debt who need help, people who need help with insurance, others who need to invest, need a savings account, need a budget sheet, some think they know everything and never took a single course on anything financial. Most people are listening to broke people like themselves and many who feel they don't need a financial coach. But they will listen to a person that gets over on them and charges them more money. Get a financial coach, some rich people and some middle- class males/females have a coach. A coach helps them make money decisions and shows them where to put their money, so it can grow to millions of dollars at retirement. Lack of knowledge, keeps us in this state of mind. Not many men/women leave their footprint of success behind. We can't make dreams come true, if you don't have a dream. Get you confidence up and build a business. Follow men/women that you know who are faithful and are true leaders. Because there are a few who are not faithful leaders. You can become a pastor (Joyce Myer), a business leader, Martin Luther King, Jr., the President (Obama), Police Officer, there are some other good ones and other powerful leaders but people just won't listen. Not everyone can be trusted, but you will know who and who not to trust. We can talk until you change colors or get blue in the face and people will not listen to powerful true role models. The people who are serious about helping others, these are the ones who get ignored the most and get disrespected because they tell the truth and other don't want to listen. Because they feel they've got everything under control, don't want people in their business, feel they make good money and need no help, have a big house, dress well and don't care to listen to anyone. People, it doesn't hurt to listen to personal advice or professional coaches. You can repeat yourself over and over, they still stay in the same spot and never change. There are many sorts out here that can help each one of us to become great. To help us with having enough retirement money, the right goals and dreams we always wanted. Many Pastors, great leaders, business partners, positive males/females, the Bible and God; all are here to show you the road to an amazing journey for a lifetime. Are you willing to grow, because many don't want to better themselves? They are content with their old habits, some complain about everything, many complain about the smallest problems but will do nothing about it. They have no intentions to improve their life. To live is to walk, in the mind of Jesus Christ, affecting the homeless, winning lost souls and being against the devil's adversity. Having an intimate relationship with God is the most powerful way to live life and keep your mind strong and stable.

# Scriptures to Help Better Your Growth

◇◇◇◇◇◇◇◇◇◇◇◇◇◇◇◇◇◇◇◇◇◇◇◇◇

1. Psalm 56:3--Whenever I am afraid, I will trust in You.
2. John 2:11—This beginning of signs Jesus did in Cana of Galilee, and manifested His glory; and His disciples believed in Him.
3. Luke 24:32—And they said to one another, Did not our heart burn within us while He talked with us on the road, and while He opened the scriptures to us?
4. 1 Peter 4:19—Therefore let those who suffer according to the will of God commit their souls to Him in doing good, as to a faithful Creator.
5. 1 Peter 5:7—casting all your cares upon Him for He cares for you.
6. 1 John 2:15—Do not love the world or the things in the world. If anyone loves the world the love of the Father is not in him.
7. Matthew 6:23—But if your eye is bad your whole body will be full of darkness. If therefore the light that is in you is darkness, how great is that darkness!
8. 1 Corinthians 2:2—For I determined not to know anything among you except Jesus Christ and Him crucified.

9. Luke 22:42—saying, Father if it is Your will, take this cup away from me nevertheless not My will but Yours, be done.
10. Isaiah 40:29---He gives power to the weak, and those who have no might. He increases strength.

# Encouraging Words

◇◇◇◇◇◇◇◇◇◇◇◇◇◇◇◇◇◇◇◇◇◇◇◇

When you know you want more, can do better financially but stay in that same old mindset, it is pointless. You have to move and fight a good fight toward your dream. Take away the fear in your life, remove those hidden secrets, the hatred, the lust in your life, it is time to begin something new and focus on all those opportunities that are available. Most of us are at home, due to the Coronavirus and now is the time to start thinking good thoughts. It's time to grow up, develop a burning desire, and be determined to hit that goal. When you believe the storm is over, you must believe God will do it, that the rain will go away, He will dry your tears and help you make it through your pain. Your eyes have been cloudy for too long from crying, your heart has been heavy but know that God is able fix it for you. With God, the family will get better, the promises God made for you, you must accept them, believe in God, believe He can heal you and you will survive, if you believe. You must believe in your heart, that things are going to get better; with your children, family, marriage, relationships and your finances. You can't give up and must bounce back.

You can look down memory lane, but bounce back. Walk in your victory and let God do it. Today is the day, wait no more and know that God has been good to you. Better than you been to yourself. Thank God for what you are going through because if you never went through anything; you would have never known that God is a good God; He's a great God and He can do anything but fail. Jesus is a Savior, way maker, healer, provider, and He knows everything about each one of us. We have a King that will never die and He is here to help you see your dreams come true. No one can take God's place, He is all we need, the one and only Deliverer. We draw near to many things in this world but have you drawn near to our King, our Savior; who will never leave us? Our boyfriend/girlfriend, husband/wife, children, mother/dad and friends walk out on us but not Jesus Christ. Stop hurting over things you have no control over. Start paying attention so you can see and hear when God speaks to you and when professional people come to give you information. They could be sent by Our Lord and Savior. Be open minded and listen to knowledge. Stop being ignorant, not knowing knowledge, not getting educated on life insurance/finances and avoid listening to people that don't have any more knowledge than you do. Life can knock you down, but get back up. We fall down but we get up. You need less of you and more of God. Are you tired of doing the same thing; doing things your way and the pain got worse? Ask God to show up and show out because you need His glory! Ask Him to show you His power and less of you. Stop crying over spilled milk and glorify God. He is moving things out of the way, will you do anything for God; more of God, more of His power, so He can give you all you need? Be around others who lift you up and encourage you, who want to see you try something new. If it's helpful for all the people in the world and meets everyone's needs, go for a dream come true. If it's something you always wanted to do, try it!

When you praise God and make Him great in your heart; the devil will flee. God is greater than your pain and your problems. When you defeat the devil and praise God, you will be able to see your vision better. Transform your mind, change your mind, remove strongholds (the past thinking behavior), change of heart and negative thinking. Stand tall, stand in authority and take back everything the devil stole from you. We have authority over the enemy. Whatever is in your life that is not of God, get away from it, remove it out of your life because you can't think clearly. Your vision is dark and you need God's love inside so your light can shine. Men/women, you don't have to put up with things that weaken your body, cause you pain, blind your vision, have you confused, worried, afraid of your heart being hurt, having you thinking you were wrong and you weren't. We all had tears that filled a river and cried so many days and nights but when God steps in, it confuses the devil. We have to praise God, bless the Lord no matter what you are feeling, praise Him when you are broke, and trouble is all around you. People don't understand it when they know you are hurting but still worship, dance, shout, and sing to Jesus. Jesus is the answer to everything. You just have to believe and know He is able to do anything. Be strong in the Lord and tough; let not the enemy easily break you, destroy you, keep you in bondage, keep you ill, have you weak but be able to endure hardship through Jesus. It is about that time to dream big, get out of the box because we don't have much time left. Stop letting people hold you back, pull you down, and making you feel you are not worthy. Be thirsty for God, on fire for Him, be committed to your Lord, be serious about having an imitate relationship with God and watch Him show up in your life. When you become stronger, better, wiser and painless, you will know it was Jesus on your side and other people prayed for you. You never would have made it without God. You would have lost your mind, if it had not been for God. Where would you like to be in the next 3 to 5 years and how much money would you like to make? You want to be set for life and at retirement. Get that vision, wake up, wake up! It's time to move.

# Scriptures for Vocabulary Words

◇◇◇◇◇◇◇◇◇◇◇◇◇◇◇◇◇◇◇◇◇◇◇◇◇

Bible Verses from the Holy Bible, the New Kings James Version. The Old and New Testaments

Afraid—Genesis 3:10 I was naked and I hid myself

Begin---Genesis 1:1 In the beginning God created

Burning---Jeremiah 20:9 Burning fire shut up in my bones

Commitment---1 Peter 4:19 Therefore let those who suffer according to the will of God commit their souls to Him in doing good as to a faithful creator.

Create----Ephesians 2:10pg 1028

Darkness----Psalm 139 Indeed the darkness shall not hide from you. Psalm 107:10 Those who sat in darkness and in the shadow of death bound in affliction and irons.

Determined---Daniel 9:24 Long, to go finish the transgression, to make an end of sins.

Fear---Psalm 27:1 The Lord is my light and my salvation, whom shall, I fear.

Focus----Colossians 3:2 Set your minds on things that are above, not the things that are on this earth. Matthews 6:33, Seek first the Kingdom of God.

Forgive---2 Ch 7:14, If my people who are called by my name will humble themselves and pray and seek my face and turn their wicked ways, then I will.....

Great---Lamentations 3:23, They are new every morning great is your faithfulness.

Hatred----Psalm 97:10, You who love the Lord, hate evil.

Hidden----Revelation 2:17, Psalm 119:11, Your word I have hidden in my heart, that I might not sin against you.

Ignorant-----2 Timothy 2:23, Avoid foolish and ignorant disputes knowing that they generate strife.

Life Style---Proverbs 8:35, For whoever finds me finds life and obtains favor from the Lord.

Listen---John 8:43, Why do you not understand My speech? Because you are not able to listen to my word.

Love---Deuteronomy 6:5, You shall love the Lord your God with all your heart, with all your soul, and with all your strength.

Mature----1 Corinthians 14:20, Philippians 3:15, Therefore let us, as many are mature have this mind; and if in anything you think otherwise, God will reveal even this to you.

Motivated----Nehemiah 8:10, Do not grieve for the joy of the Lord is your strength. Proverb 18:10, Psalm 46:1-3

Opportunities---Romans 7:8, Galatians 6:10, Therefore as we have opportunity let us do good to all, especially to those who are of the household of faith.

Pleasure---Hebrew 10:6, 10:38, Now the just shall live by faith; but if anyone draws back, my soul has no pleasure in him.

Pointless---2 Timothy 2:16,

Remove---Proverbs 30:8, Remove falsehood and lies far from me. Matthew 21:21.

Serious---Proverbs 22, 23, 24:2 and Corinthians 8

Strong---Psalm 24:8, Who is this King of glory? The Lord strong and mighty, the Lord mighty in battle.

Tough----Psalm 46:10, He says be, still and know that I am God! Exodus 14:14, The Lord will fight for you, you need only to be still.

Weak----Psalm 6:2, Have mercy on me, O Lord for I am weak; O Lord, heal me for my bones are troubled.

# Final Words

◇◇◇◇◇◇◇◇◇◇◇◇◇◇◇◇◇◇◇◇◇◇◇◇◇

Once you change your heart, your mind, and thinking, and remove some things that are in your way of seeing clearly, then you can start your vision. You can make it in life without people who don't have their best interest in you. You can do anything you want to in life or become anything. Stand up for yourself and avoid letting the devil control your thinking. Stop dwelling on the problems in your life and solve them. Many fail because they never try, some are small minded and many are still dwelling on their past hurt, for most of their whole lives. Can't move because of their feelings from a long time ago; they are filled with plenty of pain and their body stays weak and depressed. Many of us are stuck. Satan has been leading them into destruction and keeping strongholds in the mind for many years. You have a problem; wake up, wake up and get over it. Time to start a new life, with new thoughts and a vision. When you think wrong, worry, stressed, angry and unhappy; people lose their way in life. (Galatians 5:1), (Luke 8:29), You have to break all those chains off of you; stop being bitter and step out on faith. Let God help set you free from all the strongholds and worries.

It doesn't matter how you were raised or who raised you, Mom or Dad. Where you lived, whether you were poor, middle class or rich. It doesn't matter if you have done people wrong, hurt others, killed someone/something, been in and out of jail, homeless, drug user, bad attitude, make poor decisions, disrespectful, or racism. It doesn't matter, God is a God of second chances (Isaiah 43:18), (1 John 1:9), (Matthew 18:21-22), (Romans 5:8). Ask God to forgive you and you forgive yourself too. Ask Him to cleanse your body, restore your soul, give you a new heart and renew the mind. We still can change all these things in our life and do some new things. Get a new mind, new attitude, clean yourself up, and stop putting the blame on other people. Just because you lived where you lived doesn't mean you can't become great. Just because your dad wasn't there to raise you, doesn't mean you have to stay down and depressed. Just because you are in jail for whatever reason, doesn't mean you can't have a better life. We all battle with our mind, our thinking, our thoughts, and the soul man. Never give up, you are not alone.

If you are incarcerated, in jail and have no life, talk to some of the other men in jail with you and family members about writing a book. A motivated book, positive, life story, heartfelt book, for men/women and boys/girls so they don't have to experience what you have been through. Your book may help others, may save a life, you can be a witness or your book can be a testimony for thousands of men/women. Some men have been in jail for years (over 15 years or more) for no reason and didn't do the crime. That was terrible sitting in prison knowing you are innocent but couldn't prove it. You had to just keep praying and fighting to get out. When a person comes up years later and confesses they did the crime, something must have been really eating them up inside (their conscience must be eating he/she alive) and you been in jail for years. But God bless you, you got out and survived in jail. But that was unfair to you. You can write a book on that and how your loved ones believed you and kept fighting for you too. How you got your freedom back? Tell your story; everyone has a story to tell. You see, you can reach out and still touch many people's lives. Try to help make this world a better and safer place. God isn't finished with you yet. He wants to use you too; for His glory. God takes the foolish things in this world, sinners, and makes good out of them, (1 Corinthians 1:27). We all are sinners and have failed; we have failed a loved one, yourself, other people and God (Romans 3:23). But that is not an excuse for not changing your life around from being bitter; try the joy of the Lord and His love. We fall down but we get up; we fall down but we get back up again and again. You still can work toward a vision, goal or dream; get your mind right with the Lord. Think about your, why? Why I'm I acting like this or why should I do this for me and my family? WHY?

# The Author

◇◇◇◇◇◇◇◇◇◇◇◇◇◇◇◇◇◇◇◇◇◇◇◇

Susan Sykes is a wife and a mother of two children, a boy and a girl, and a granddaughter, six step children and other grandkids. Born in Virginia but raised in Baltimore, Maryland, Susan graduated from High School, went to college for childcare, graduated from Bible School, has her license for life insurance and other licenses. She enjoys walking, playing basketball, likes playing tennis and likes baseball. She would like to thank Jesus Christ for saving her and loving her. Mrs. Sykes want to share how important it is to make Jesus Christ, 1st in your life and also have a goal/vision. Susan loves people, enjoys giving encouraging words, likes helping people and sharing God's word and His love, with all. He has blessed her and she is grateful to spread the Father's love everywhere she goes. Many who come in contact with her can feel her warm spirit and personality. They open up to her with their problems. It is something they see inside of her which makes them feel comfortable with sharing some of their personal information. Mrs. Sykes share her thoughts from the word of God, which is the Bible. What the Bible means to her is: Basic Instruction before Leaving This Earth. Susan doesn't know where she would be right now, if it had not been for the Lord on her side. Whatever you are going through, go to God, in prayer for help and for your vision. You are not alone.

This book is to help the world overcome hatred, violence/killing, all unforgiving spirits and leave the past behind. It can't be undone because it happened already. We all need to be loved by God, learn His agape kind of love which is unconditional and love no matter what has happened now and in the past. Please wake up, see that you are making your problem worse, by dwelling on who hurt you and playing the blame game. Just because someone hurt you, you don't have to stay angry or continue to harm others. Please don't block your dreams come true or your vision. Many people are struggling, so why try to hurt someone you once loved because they weren't there for you or because they are with another man/woman. Don't you have enough problems on your plate! You are digging a deeper hole for yourself. Is that really what you want? Relationships and marriage are real, you go through ups and down. They both can either broke a person or make them stronger. They both can make you have a happy/great life or miserable/sad life. Make your attitude better or worse, it also can make you harm yourself or live life in victory. Victory is mine, victory is mine, victory today is mine, now tell Satan to move out of your life and get out of your home. We have the authority over Satan, the Bible tells us! We must take that stand and speak it out loud. Take back everything the devil stole from you, your peace of mind, joy, father, husband, wife, children, vision, hope, attitude, praise, your family, worship, go back to church, get the house in order, and return to the Savior. He is able to keep us from falling. Let Him have full control of your body, He is the love that you are searching for. No one can do you the way Jesus Christ can! Forgive, Love and Get a Vision. Never put your faith in people, only Jesus Christ. People will fail you every time. Just because you fail doesn't mean you are a failure. You fail when you stop trying and give up. Jesus, He won't let you down, He won't break your heart and He won't let you fall, so give everything to Him. Jesus did it for Susan Sykes and He will do it for you. Let Him enter into your life, come into your heart and love you like you never been loved before. We all need an intimate relationship with Jesus Christ. A friend to the end. AMEN.

# TIPS—BE AWARE

◇◇◇◇◇◇◇◇◇◇◇◇◇◇◇◇◇◇◇◇◇◇◇◇◇

Women, please recognize what the devil tries to speak to your brain and put in your heart. Avoid opening your legs too fast to all different kinds of men. Never do something with a man, if you don't want to. Just because they say something nice to you doesn't mean spread your legs. Learn to be friends with a man first, because not all men are your type, some are there to only be a good friend to you. The men that only see you at night, have to take you out of town, where no one knows him or you and keep you hidden, he's no good for you? He's only using you. Leave him alone. If he doesn't want to take pictures with you or be seen in daylight with you, leave him. If he tells you he loves you, and always come around at night, something is wrong. Watch out for these signs that make you feel a man is cheating or has someone else. They are clear signs but you being in denial, don't want to believe it. When a man leaves you and you haven't talked to him for weeks or longer, let him be and don't let him back in your life. No man leaves a woman he loves for weeks/years and you have no clue whose bed he is in and blocks your number. You aren't married to him, that is why he does as he pleases. Stop sleeping with these men and you know you are not the only one.

You love that man so much, that he is very guilty of loving you because he has someone special in his life. You are doing things to a man that he is not getting at home or he can be getting it at home but wants his cake and eat it too. Just because a man might take you to see his family, mother or father doesn't mean anything, if he's not doing you right and he gives you reason to believe that it's other women. Leave him! Women, stop letting men tell you anything and you accept it. He's not the only man that lied to you; this has been going on, your whole life. You need God because no one else can help you. The person you talk about all the time has full control over your life. Stop talking about the same old no good person or man.

One minute you talk about how in love you are and the next couple of days you crying because you think he is with someone else. Putting it on social media makes you look crazy. You talk bad about the man then take up for him; you are a confused woman and need help. Women, your friends can't help you because when they tell you the truth, you refuse to listen. You don't want to hear the truth because you are in love. There are some women who accept anything that comes their way because they have low self-esteem. They feel that they need a man, got to have a man, all the men have used her, can't keep a man because you open your legs too fast, or many of you are used to being used. Do you like feeling bad and being mistreated?

Many men can tell what women they can use, a soft woman, a woman who doesn't speak what's on her mind, women who hold everything inside, a slow woman/person, a woman who he can get sex from fast and have her doing all kinds of treats to him. He just wanted to feel good for a few minutes and out the door he goes. There are men who come over to your place and stay for two hours, leave early before the sun come up, and won't take you to work; you caught the bus. We must stop sleeping with men who don't give you a dime. They come to your house when they want, don't help the woman pay any bills, don't help take care of her kids, some have keys to your home and whenever the man comes over it's a big surprise or Christmas. That is just how happy women are over these men, that don't care nothing about them and they don't treat you like Queens. Some ladies don't give their own children that much attention!

Many women have been abused by men in front of their children but keep taking that man back. If a man hits you, that is not love because one day he is going to seriously take you out of this world.

Women/Men feel they need someone, are afraid to be alone, and feel they need sex. That is the wrong way to think, if you are looking for a long-life relationship. The way you carry yourself is how you are going to get treated. Men cheat and have beautiful women at home and if their women only knew what some of their men were out here sleeping with and bringing home diseases! Some men have good looking wives and girlfriends but still cheat.

Women get lied to right in front of their face but because they missed him and haven't seen him in weeks, she just accepts the lie. The two head straight to that bed, as if nothing happen. Time to get that feel good on and forget about that lie. When are we going to stop letting these men keep us down? When are you going to see that your children need you and you can do much better? Is he that good, that he takes your breath away and stop you from your goals and career? You keep stopping because a man hurt you? No one is going to push you or hold your hand; you must finish what you start. Some men don't like a woman who just sits home all day, doing nothing. Yes, he's going to sleep with you but he's also going to mess around on you. You can never watch or keep an eye on a person 24/7, unless you tie them up. You women need to find something to do and become success. Chasing behind a man only holds you back from doing something amazing for you and your children. I know you love him but the pain; are you sick of all that stress? You have to wake up one day.

Being a fool in love, is foolish. It's a time to mature and grow up. Many of us are grown but are lost in love and don't want to leave. Women, listen, take the advice and make a move, when your best friend tells you the truth about yourself. Don't be mad, you get mad with the wrong people but a man can destroy you and you still love him. So sad! Believe it or not, there is a man out there but you won't get him until you get out of that messed up relationship. If you aren't married, stop crying over a person that's not yours. Take time out for a while and years later find a new love, baby, a new love. Many of you don't know how much better you will feel, once you leave that bad relationship. You will have so much freedom, your mind will be clear, your heart will rejoice, your kids will be happy, and you can do great things and make yourself some money. And one day have a business, but you haven't been able to focus for years and years. You are not alone, but it's time to move. Time is running out and you've been in the grave for too long. It's your time to come alive and live your dream.

Some women just want to be loved but are searching in all the wrong places. A desperate woman, that takes anything that comes her way or a man whisper in her ear. "I like your eyes, you look good, you are fine, you are fat and your shape I just love." Some men are lying to some of you woman but you know if you got it going on because you don't settle for anything. There are some women who don't look good and will settle for less all the time, and you do have some pretty ladies that men use too. They know what to say and how to get a woman with the words that come out of their mouth. They enjoy sweet talking ladies and women like a man to say, "I love you." You are really in love now but they disrespect you. You don't trust him, and are unhappy. What a waste of time and life. You can't get that time back but you can feel better, if you choose to.

A man that acts worse than a woman and likes to argue. Leave him alone because he needs a lot of growing up to do. He is still drinking milk. You are too mature for him. Women, if you are stressed out, beating yourself up, depressed all the time, and worrying over a man that doesn't care about you: Get over it and move on. So many women have sickness, cancer, depression, are hurting, holding silence in their heart, and lost hair because for years men have used them. Many women can find time to be depressed but can't find time to become a success to themselves and others. Men that keep your relationship secret; get rid of him. If he really wants you and knows that you are the one for him, he won't care who knows about you and him because you will be the one he wants to spend the rest of his life with. Avoid being a bootie call. Women why let people stop you from making more money? Let them go; if you are grown, you should be making your own decisions.

Women who stay on your cell phone, gossip about men, always have problems and tell all your business. Stop it because people hate negative conversations every day and all day long. Grow you! That is why you can't get things done. You have your mind set on the wrong things and is filled with negative thinking. If your mind is on just men and sex, you will not reach your dreams come true. You block your own blessing because the men don't have a gun to your head to make you stay with them. That's your decision. Stop using your money and body as a tool to get a man because that is what most of them want anyway. So, if you want to be used, that's what a man is going to do. Sleep with you and dump you. If you are giving him money too, he's going to take it. If you have a child and someone else is raising that child, you need to get yourself focused. Take care of your child or children, you need help! Anytime you put a man before your children, your priorities are in the wrong place.

There are women who meet a guy for the first day and claim she got a man. It is not all of us but something is really wrong with a woman like this. Don't know this person at all and will sleep with any man who sweet talks her ears off. A woman that gives men money, hasn't known them long and that is all the men want from her and a little sex. Avoid these things. Many men like stupid women, but not all men. Avoid sleeping with a married man and thinking he is your man because he goes home to his wife every night. Why do you think he never sleeps over your house or spends the whole day with you? Get rid of all the wrong men in your life and maybe you can think better and feel better.

If your man sees that you really need help with something and he doesn't give you money. Why are you still with him? You all should want to be treated like a Queen! Be smart and know when you are being used. Learn to be alone, clear your mind, worry about you and your health. Take your mind off of a man for a while. You've been going around in circles for years. He's got you going in circles, round and round you go and you are strung out over him. Stop being a sucker for these men who are doing you wrong. You are just a sucker for his love. If he isn't loving you, who in the world is he loving? Tell him you don't need him around and that he is going to make you love somebody else if he keeps on treating you the way he does. To overcome these bad relationships, we all are going to need Jesus Christ. That is the answer to all our problems, the key and your ultimate peace of mind.

Get a Vision and Dream Big Dreams

Time
to think about
SUCCESS

Printed in the United States
by Baker & Taylor Publisher Services